WITHDRAWN

# The Bad Samaritan

# *The Bad Samaritan*

• A NOVEL OF SUSPENSE •
• FEATURING CHARLIE PEACE •

## Robert Barnard

Thorndike Press • Chivers Press
Thorndike, Maine USA • Bath, Avon, England

This Large Print edition is published by Thorndike Press, USA and by Chivers Press, England.

Published in 1996 in the U.S. by arrangement with Scribner, an imprint of Simon & Schuster, Inc.

Published in 1996 in the U.K. by arrangement with HarperCollins Publishers.

U.S.  Hardcover 0-7862-0563-6  (Cloak & Dagger Series Edition)
U.K.  Hardcover 0-7451-7985-1  (Windsor Large Print)

Thorndike Large Print® Cloak & Dagger Series.

The text of this Large Print edition is unabridged.
Other aspects of the book may vary from the original edition.

Set in 16 pt. News Plantin.

Printed in the United States on permanent paper.

---

British Library Cataloguing in Publication Data available

---

Library of Congress Cataloging in Publication Data

Barnard, Robert.
    The bad samaritan / Robert Barnard.
        p.   cm.
    ISBN 0-7862-0563-6 (lg. print : hc)
    1. Large type books.   I. Title.
[PR6052.A665B3   1996]
823.'914—dc20                                    95-33649

*For*
*Margaret Burton,*
*who knows the problems*

# Part I

## *Rosemary*

# CHAPTER ONE

# *A Loss*

*R*osemary Sheffield backed her husband's car out of the garage and through the gates, then parked it by the side of the road pointing in the direction of St Saviour's. She got out, blinking in the early spring sunshine. Feeling rather silly she dabbed with a cloth at the door handles. For some reason she could not fathom, her husband was fussy about the appearance of his car when he went off to take service. It was presumably a form of vanity, since in other respects he had no illusions about cleanliness being next to godliness. Anyway, there it was waiting for him: clean, sleek and shining.

Her husband sailed out, clerical collar gleaming white over pale grey, folder clutched in his hand. From time to time the folder exploded, scattering all over the driveway, and when that happened, and they scrabbled together on the driveway bumping heads, Rosemary had to tell herself she wouldn't have wanted an orderly husband. Today the folder remained intact. Her husband pecked her on the cheek.

"I'll be there tonight, Paul," Rosemary said, and he nodded, put the car into gear and drove smoothly away. He loves that car, Rosemary thought, though without any feeling of jealousy. The sun felt warm on her cheek, wonderful after the long, bleak winter months. She felt she ought to go indoors and get down to things, particularly as she had told Paul how busy she was. Instead, relishing the clear morning light, she crossed the road on to the grassy open spaces of Herrick Park.

The turf felt good under her thin-soled shoes. There were the usual dog-walkers, and she thought again it was time to get another dog: getting a puppy immediately after Bo'sun had died had seemed wrong to her, a sort of unfaithfulness, though everyone had said it was the only way to get over her grief. She still missed him, missed their walks and games together. If it had happened when the children were still young, there would have been more to take her mind off it. She looked over to the tennis courts, where two students were playing a strenuous, rough and ready game. In the distance she saw one of the usual Sunday morning joggers approaching.

And suddenly, in the warmth, surrounded by shimmering light, she felt something lift from her, leave her. It was as if a worry had suddenly evaporated — she could almost physically feel herself being rid of it. She said to herself: "I do not believe." There was no need to add to the sentence. There was nothing to add. Suddenly she knew that she no longer believed. She had lost her faith. She stood there feeling free and happy — feeling, indeed, almost lightheaded. She no longer believed in God: not the Christian God, not any God. She felt she ought to feel desolate, deprived, but she didn't: she felt liberated, joyful, full of the most enormous potential. The road ahead of her seemed suddenly wider, taking her through an entirely different landscape.

The jogger approached down the path from the woods. It was a young black man she had seen often in the park. She raised her hand and he raised his in return. As he passed her she was conscious that he was looking at her curiously. She ought to feel bad about that: clergymen's wives should not do anything that made people look at them curiously. But she did not turn and go back into the house. She stood there in the godless sun, savouring her new freedom.

When she thought about it later in the morning, going about her accumulation of tasks, she realised that her loss of faith could not have come suddenly, as it had seemed. It must have been led up to, must have been the culmination of a process involving worries, niggling doubts, shifts in patterns of thinking. But, puzzle as she might, she could not remember any occasion when doubt had tried to force a way into her mind and had been repressed. There had been no incident — no accident or massacre, no personal loss — where she had questioned whether a benign God would allow such a thing to happen. So then and later Rosemary saw her loss of faith as a sudden thing, a quite unexpected *lifting*, as if she was standing on a mountain and suddenly the cloud had gone, revealing wonderful new perspectives.

As usual she timed the Sunday lunch for two. Paul sometimes went off for a pint with some of his male parishioners after the service, or liked time for a sherry at home with her — something, anyhow, to relax him after the tensions of taking the service, for tensions, even after all these years, there still were. As she peeled and scraped she meditated the totally unexpected questions: When would she tell him? How would he take the news? The first question was easily answered: not

12

until after he'd enjoyed the pork, his favourite roast. The second question was not easily answered at all. She felt she simply didn't know. That was odd, after all these years of marriage, parenthood, and the usual vicissitudes of modern life. She felt she knew her husband very well, but this was a totally unexplored terrain, and she lacked a compass. She trusted Paul and loved him, but this . . .

The pork was tender, the roast potatoes crisp as he liked them, the peas just like frozen peas always are. Even with just the two of them there was an air of well-being hovering over the table. After pudding, a bread-and-butter one, and when she had put cheese and biscuits on the table, Paul said he could do no more than toy with them.

"Wonderful meal," he said. "I would say I've had an elegant sufficiency, but I've had a good deal more than that."

Rosemary smiled, her mind working away.

"Who went along to the Game Cock with you?"

"Oh, Jim Russell, Arthur Beeston and Dark Satanic Mills."

"What did *he* want?"

Her husband smiled tolerantly.

"You always ask that. The poor man's been coming to church for nearly fifteen years and you still suspect his motives."

"I certainly do. I won't say 'You've only got to look at him' because I know how you'll react."

Paul Sheffield nodded.

"I'll say you have a conventional as well as a suspicious mind."

"Questioning, anyway. . . . A funny thing happened to me today, Paul."

"That sounds like the beginning of a bad joke."

"No, it's not. . . . Or I don't think so." She swallowed. Now for it. "After you drove off to service I went for a little walk in the park, it was so nice."

"It *was* nice, wasn't it? Lucky you."

"And I suddenly realised . . . that I don't *believe* any longer."

Her husband's mouth dropped, just as he was about to pop a piece of crumbly cheese into it.

"You're joking."

"Not at all."

He put the cheese down and swallowed. "You mean you've lost your faith?"

"Yes."

"Rosie, how awful for you."

She left a pause before she answered.

"Maybe. But oddly enough it doesn't feel awful."

"How does it feel?"

"Liberating. As if a cloud has lifted."

Paul frowned. He's quite bewildered, the poor lamb, thought Rosemary.

"But your faith and the Church are so important in your life, so central. Surely you must feel . . . empty?"

"I would have expected to, if I'd thought about it, but I don't." She added carefully: "perhaps it was the Church that was central, rather than the faith."

"We must all try and help you as much as we can."

"I won't have you publicly praying for the return of my faith, Paul."

"No, of course not, if you feel like that," he said hurriedly. Then he added, with a quick glance at her: "perhaps it would be better not to say anything at all about it for the moment."

Rosemary considered.

"Maybe you're right. I don't want to make it a dark little secret. On the other hand, to announce it does seem to give *me* a lot more importance than I actually have."

"A lot of people in the parish will be very upset. And the children will be."

"Oh, the children are tougher than you think — children have to be these days. Janet will probably imagine it's my time of life, knowing her, and Mark certainly will pray for me. I only hope he keeps *quiet* about it, that's all."

"Perhaps you need time off — time away."

She frowned at him.

"You're not trying to get rid of me, are you, Paul?"

"No, of course I'm not."

"Shuffle me out of the way, so that people don't *talk*. You're horribly afraid of people *talking*."

"I don't like people talking nonsense, which you are now."

"Because eventually the parish is going to have to know, and then they're going to talk."

"I'm sure everyone will be very sympathetic."

"Golly yes — that's what I'm dreading. And those will be the nice ones, not the troublemakers."

"But you're talking as if it's gone for good and is never going to come back."

"You make it sound like a skin disease."

"Well, is it gone for good?"

Rosemary pondered.

"I really don't know. How could I know? How could anyone? It *feels* that way, that's all I know. I suppose it may *descend* on me again as suddenly as it lifted. But I have to say I don't expect it to."

"Will you come to church?"

"I'll come tonight, as I said I would. I'll see how it feels. I'm not sure I want to *pretend* to pray."

"You could just close your eyes."

"That *would* be pretending to pray. Anyway, people know how I pray. People notice me — as the vicar's wife. More's the pity. One of the things I hate about Dark Satanic Mills is the way he looks at me."

"What about the Harvest Festival Committee and the Mothers' Union meeting?"

"Oh, I won't have any problem with the social side. Why should I? They're all quite useful activities, or pleasant enough. I'll do them as your wife, as I've always done."

"That's a relief. I do think you ought to keep coming to church as well. It might help."

Rosemary laughed.

"You show a touching confidence in your own powers as a spiritual leader," she teased him.

"You know I don't mean that. I mean the experience — the prayers, the hymns, the communion."

"Of course I'll have to stop taking communion. Then everybody will know."

"Yes, they'll know then."

"And *won't* there be whispering!"

Paul Sheffield looked very unhappy. The

17

uncharted territory that seemed exciting to Rosemary only bewildered him. He had always been a consolidator rather than an explorer.

It was certainly an odd experience going to church that evening. As usual, there were far fewer there than at Holy Communion — fewer to notice, Rosemary thought. She sang the hymns enthusiastically: she was a would-be choral singer who could imagine no joy greater than singing in the *Messiah* or the *Sea Symphony* but had somehow always failed in her attempts to learn to read music. But for the rest it was going through a charade — quite empty. She occupied her mind with thought: had it been going towards this for some time? Had religious observance gradually had its significance drained out of it for her? She had certainly not been conscious of it if so. There seemed all the difference in the world between her participation in Holy Communion the Sunday before and the pantomime performance which was all she could manage now — like an actor playing his part in an empty theatre.

But the thing that struck her most was that she did *not* feel empty, did not feel a sense of loss or deprivation. She felt good; she felt stimulated; she felt free. Have I been living a lie all these years, she wondered? Can one

18

live a lie without knowing it? Can one think one believes when in reality one doesn't? What was she going to say to Paul about the service? She imagined him asking her, "How was it for you?" and had to suppress a giggle. She looked round to see if anyone had noticed, and rather suspected that Mrs Harridance had.

After the service she waited for Paul by the car. He stood in the porch exchanging pleasantries, parish small talk and gossip with the members of his congregation. In the past she would normally have stopped with him and participated in the chat, but tonight she felt awkward. He's a good parish priest, thought Rosemary, looking at him. I hope this doesn't spoil things for him. Of course logically there was no reason at all why it should, but logic wasn't always operative in parish affairs.

Paul freed himself from his little knot of admirers and came over to let himself and her into the car. He put it into gear and drove off towards home.

"Did the service do anything for you?" he asked. Again she had to suppress a giggle.

"Absolutely nothing. Do you realise you're sounding like a doctor again?"

"Sorry. It's obviously going to be a long process."

"If there is a process at all. I think it's something I and everyone else are just going to have to accept."

Paul looked genuinely upset.

"Oh, I hope not."

"I'm beginning to feel *observed* — do you know what I mean?"

"Not entirely."

"Beginning to feel that people — you mainly, of course, but the sharper-eyed parish members as well — are observing me, as if they know I've got something terminal and they're watching for symptoms of my approaching demise."

"You're being absurd. Nobody knows. And who's talking in medical terms now?"

"I know I am. . . . Still, I think I *might* go away after all."

That cheered Paul up.

"I do think it might be a good idea. We can afford it."

"Oh, I wouldn't go to anywhere grand. But I could think things out without any of the people I know watching me."

"The Lakes?"

"Hmmm. I don't think so. I'd feel Auntie Wordsworth looking over my shoulder and telling me to experience God through nature. I think the sea would suit me better. Brid or Scarborough. There wouldn't be anyone much there at this time of year."

"What will you do?"

"Walk on the beach, walk on the cliffs, sew, read a detective story, put flowers on Anne Brontë's grave."

"Scarborough, then?"

"Yes, Scarborough, I think. There's more to do there if the weather is vile."

"And you'll . . . think things over?"

She patted his arm.

"Yes, I'll think things over. But you can't *think* yourself into a faith, you know."

"I'm sure many people have done just that."

"Not me. That wouldn't be my kind of faith."

He left it there. They had a cosy, joky evening together, with television and music. When they went to bed Rosemary was afraid she was going to get the feeling that Paul was praying for her, but if he did he did it discreetly. They made love and he was as warm and tender as he had ever been. In the morning Rosemary looked in her address book and rang a guesthouse they had stayed at three summers before on St Nicholas's Cliff in Scarborough. She felt perhaps she ought to feel cowardly, as if making a strategic withdrawal. Instead she had an exhilarating sense of going off to pastures new.

★ ★ ★

"Have you ever known anyone have a mystical experience?" Charlie Peace asked his superior Mike Oddie, as he slogged his way through a mountain of paperwork in the CID offices at Leeds Police Headquarters the next morning.

"Can't say I have. What does a mystical experience consist of?"

"I'm not sure I know."

"Why do you ask?"

"Because I saw a woman in the park yesterday, and it looked as if that was what she was going through."

"What did it look like?"

"Like she'd had a revelation. Like she'd suddenly discovered God."

"Bully for her," said Mike.

"Only I don't think it was that."

"Why?"

"Because I think she's a clergyman's wife."

## CHAPTER TWO

# A Friend

*R*osemary walked from the Scarborough station to her guesthouse. The journey had been uneventful, except that on Leeds station she had bumped into Dark Satanic Mills, who had leered at her as if he knew something about her — a knowing, conspiratorial look that she had tried to freeze but failed. Her case was not large or heavy because she did not see her holiday as an opportunity for a display of fashion, even had she had the wherewithal for one, so walking the short distance was no problem. She did notice as she loitered along that there were shops in Scarborough that sold the sort of clothes that she liked. She wondered whether she might take the opportunity to branch out into an entirely different sort of clothes, but she decided it was too late. It was not a change of *life* she was embarking on, but a change of *thought*. Anyway, now was hardly the time to start feeling uneasy about what she was wearing.

Scarborough was mildly bustling in a watery, uncertain sunshine, and Rosemary congratulated herself on picking it. Bridlington would have been dull at this time of year. Brid was dull at any time of year. At Scarborough there was usually plenty going on.

It was lunchtime when she arrived at the Cliff View Guesthouse, set in a commanding position on St Nicholas's Cliff opposite the bricky horrors of the Grand Hotel. The proprietress welcomed her as someone she already knew, said she'd given her one of the bedrooms with a sea view, and asked if she would be taking lunch. Rosemary had had a tasteless sandwich on the train and shook her head.

"I expect I'll generally have dinner as my main meal," she said, having booked half board. "It fits in better with my husband's work to have the main meal in the evening, so that's what I've got used to."

"Isn't your husband a clergyman?"

"That's right."

"Awfully demanding on their wives, I've always thought."

"Yes. . . . Yes, I've never thought about it, but I suppose it is. Restricting, certainly."

24

"Anyway, you can forget it for a bit and enjoy yourself, can't you?"

"Oh, I expect I'll have a very quiet time."

Rosemary took her case up to her room, which did indeed have the most splendid view out to sea. That was the joy of coming out of season: you got the best rooms. She unpacked everything and set out things as if she had come for a long stay.

Once she had freshened up she went out to the shops. She just browsed in the clothes shops, but in the bookshop she bought a biography of the Sitwells and a detective story set in ancient Rome. "I'm here to think, not to shop," she chided herself. "No I'm not," the other side of her mind said, "I'm here to get away from people." No part of her said, "I'm here to regain my faith." She took the funicular down to the beach and had a long walk along the headland. She must have been thinking as she walked but, oddly enough, when she got back to the Cliff View Guesthouse she had no idea what it was she had been thinking about.

She took a book in to dinner that night. It was the sort of place where you could, and eating alone is never easy. You wait, try not to look around, and hope the other diners aren't feeling sorry for you. She was just beginning to enjoy the manifest impossibility of the Sitwells' father (as one does enjoy on the printed page people one would run a mile from in life) when she felt a shadow at her shoulder.

"You like the meat or the fish? The meat is pork fillet and the fish is salmon. Is also a veg'tarian dish, but is not nice if you not veg'tarian."

"I can imagine," said Rosemary. "Or even if you are one, probably. I'll have pork."

He smiled, as if that was what he would have advised if he had been allowed to guide her choice. When he came with the meal Rosemary found it was indeed the sort of meal she might have cooked herself at home. She put aside her book and looked around her. The dining room was sparsely peopled: two middle-aged couples and three elderly ones, three other single ladies and one single man. The waiter was managing to cope on his own, banging happily in and out of the swing doors leading to the kitchen.

After she had enjoyed the pork, Rosemary took up her book again and managed to continue reading while eating a remarkably boring fruit salad. She congratulated herself on choosing a place where you could do the kind of thing that you did when you were at home without disapproving eyes being fixed on you. Rosemary was just finishing her coffee when the waiter darted up to her from the foyer, a question in his dark eyes.

"You Meesa Sheffield? There phone call for you. Thees way."

Rosemary followed him, thinking it must be Paul, then realised he would be at a Parochial Church Council meeting. When she picked up the phone in the foyer it was her daughter's voice she heard.

"Hello Mum. We wondered how you were."

That medical metaphor again, as if spiritual and physical health were inextricably muddled in everyone's mind but her own. How much did Janet know?

"Hello Janet. Lovely to hear from you. Who's 'we'?"

"Kevin and I, of course. And Mark is here as well."

"Good Lord." Her daughter and her son Mark never fought, but they had never seemed to have much in common and seldom got together except at home. "What are you two cooking up?"

"Just got tickets for *Carousel*, that's all. Mum — Dad says you're going through some kind of crisis."

"I'm sure he told you exactly what kind of crisis, dear, so there's no point in beating about the bush. Actually I'm not sure I regard

27

it as a crisis at all."

"Well, it's your life, Mum. I hope you manage to think things through. We wanted you to know we're right behind you."

"That's good of you, dear."

"Mark wants a word."

Why did her heart sink?

"Mum?"

"Hello, Mark dear. I do hope you all enjoy *Carousel*."

"I'm sure we will. Mum — you've really got to work at this thing, you know."

Rosemary was conscious of a sharp but not unexpected twinge of irritation. It wasn't just being told what to do by her son. It was the quality and tone of her son's voice: the quality was plummy and the tone was — what? Condescending? Forbearing of human frailty? Parsonical in the worst sense?

"Oh?" she said coldly.

"You mustn't think your faith will just return, you know. You've got to work at it — pray hard, think things through, try to work out where you've gone wrong to make God leave you in this terrible way."

"Thank you, Mark. I think I have things under control. I should have thought even you would have realised that it's not easy to pray when you have no one and nothing to pray to. Don't let me keep you from *Carousel*."

And she put the phone down, feeling angrier than she had done in years. What had she and Paul done to produce a sermonising prat like Mark, and him only twenty-two years old? She retrieved her book from the empty dining room and wandered into the lounge. *The Bill* was on, watched by a bored and uncomprehending elderly guest. She sat down, but found the television did nothing to soothe her fuming mind. Drug trafficking on a run-down and violent Council estate was not a restful subject. There was a bookcase in the corner with a lot of old Companion Bookclub books in it, and a few standard classics. She didn't feel like starting a new detective story — she always read fiction before she went to bed — so she went over, inspected the stock, and took out *A Tale of Two Cities*. She hadn't read it, to her recollection, since she was at college. It wasn't as soothing as a Jane Austen, but she felt she wasn't cool enough for sly Jane.

On the landing she was caught up with by the slim waiter, bounding up the stairs.

"You have nice telephone call?"

"Yes thank you," she lied. "It was my son and daughter."

"Very nice." He paused, and then said:

"I have a little girl — back in Bosnia."

"Oh dear — how awful for you. Are you Bosnian?"

He shrugged.

"Bosnian, Serbian, Croatian — what does it matter? I thought I was Yugoslavian."

"Do you get news from your wife?"

"I not talk to her for many weeks — months. Is no lines. Sometimes I have letter from my wife, but not often." He patted the breast pocket of his jacket. "I not talk about my problems no more. You here on holiday."

"I'm very interested, er — sorry, I don't know your name."

"They call me Stan here."

Rosemary was about to say that didn't sound very romantic, but she thought she might give the wrong impression, so she simply said, "Good night, Stan," and watched him open an unmarked door and bound up the poky stairs to his room in the attic.

The next morning, after a leisurely breakfast in which she admired Stan's dexterity with five or six plates and his excellent memory for orders of great complexity, Rosemary walked down to the lower part of the town. Here she could see the other Scarborough: whelk stalls, fortune-tellers, amusement arcades and streets littered with takeaway cartons. Come the summer holidays and there would be people in funny hats with slogans on them, fat women in skimpy cheap dresses, screaming children with snotty noses. "There is nothing for me here," Rosemary said to herself and walked on to the beach and down to the sea's edge.

The sea should have put her in mind of eternal things, but it did not. She was niggling away at her previous thought: *why* had the lower town nothing for her? It was a loud, vulgar, happy kind of place in its way, yet she shrank from it, hated the harsh music with the heavy bass issuing from the arcades, hated the misspelt and mispunctuated hand-painted advertisements and shop signs. Here am I, a vicar's wife, she thought, someone who ought to be in touch with all sorts of people. But the sort of people who come on day trips here in summer are totally alien to me — or if not alien at least foreign. There are no people like that at St Saviour's — there are in the parish, but they don't come to church. Of Paul's parishioners the people I like and the people I dislike — Dark Satanic Mills and Mrs Harridance, for example — are all middle-class. Am I simply a snob? And if so have I always been one, or have I been made one by Paul's congregation?

She was struck by a horrible thought: people seeing me here, standing by the water's edge, could probably guess that I am a vicar's wife. I dress like a vicar's wife: sensible jumper and skirt, with flat or low-heeled shoes. I have my hair done like a vicar's wife: sensibly tied back so as not to need too much attention. I make up like a vicar's wife: very discreetly. I am a vicar's wife *type*. I can be pigeonholed.

Disturbed, she turned and walked in the direction of St Nicholas's Cliff.

She walked very slowly, keeping close to the sea, stopping now and then to look at the boats. How much more activity, she thought, there would have been out to sea in Anne Brontë's time. And when the Sitwells used to spend their summers here as children. She reached the bottom of the funicular railway and was just wondering whether it was warm enough to sit and read for a bit before finding somewhere for a sandwich and a cup of coffee when she saw the figure of Stan, sitting on an anorak spread out on the sand, gazing abstractedly out to sea.

He looked slight, sad and very vulnerable. Her heart was touched by pity for him, and she felt maternal in a way she could no longer feel for her own son. He was so far from home and so terribly separated from his loved ones. How could one explain what was going on in Yugoslavia? How could European, educated, civilized people do such things to each other? What did it feel like to be one of these people and to have loved ones caught up in the conflict? She found she could not stop herself going over and sitting beside him.

"Hello," she said. "It's a lovely day, isn't it?"

He looked up at her and smiled shyly.

"Yes, lovely. For England."

"Would you rather be home in Bosnia?"

"No!" He said it violently, and there was fear in his voice too. "How could I want to be there when things are as they are now? But I would like very much my family here with me."

"Of course."

"I would even like to know where they are."

"You don't know that?"

"No. The last I hear, they are in a camp, my wife and little girl. But that was nearly three months ago. And it was not very far from the fighting. You see why I am so worried?" He shrugged. "What people we are."

"*How* can that kind of thing happen today?" asked Rosemary passionately. He shrugged again.

"It go back to the war. More back, to when we became Yugoslavia. More back, to the Austrian Empire. More back, more back. Too

33

much history, too many people, too much religions. We all have — what is the word? — things we want revenges for."

"Grudges."

"Grudges, yes. We have so many. We want to pay back things our fathers suffered, things our grandfathers suffered. Too many peoples, too much history."

Rosemary thought it all sounded much like Scottish history in Stuart times. Or Irish history at any time since the Settlements. To change the subject she said, "Have you got a picture of your little girl?"

He nodded, dived into the pocket of his threadbare jacket and shuffled through a pile of snapshots in his bulging wallet. He handed a picture to her. It was a baby in white at its christening, a crucifix in the background.

"She looks lovely. . . . Are you a Christian?"

"Oh yes. But my grandmother is Moslem. We are a bit of everything in my family. Is true of many families in Bosnia. That is what is so mad, you see: when we fight each other we also fight part of ourselves."

He put the snapshot tenderly back in the pile of memories and stood up.

"I must go and get ready for lunch. I have one hour free only in morning."

"They work you hard."

He shook his head.

"Is good. I not complain. It stop me thinking."

"Thank you for talking to me, Stan. . . .
Do I have to call you Stan? It's a slightly
ridiculous name. No young man is called Stan
these days."

"I am Stanko. Call me Stanko."

"That's better. I'm Rosemary."

"You not come to lunch, Rosemary?"

"No, I'm on half board. I prefer dinner."

"Is sensible. Lunch is often offle!"

He raised his hand and disappeared into
the tiny station just above the beach. Rosemary stayed on the rock, looking out to sea.
She did not take out her book, but for some
reason her thoughts strayed to her reading
of the night before: to Dr Manette reverting
at moments of crisis to the shoemaking he
had done for years during his long incar-
ceration. This had reminded her of things
learnt at teachers college: of Dickens's own
obsessive returning, over and over in the
books, to his months in the blacking ware-
house. We are all prisoners of the most terrible times in our past, she thought. The child
victims of sex abuse, the adult victims of rape,
seem never able to put it behind them. What
chance was there for Yugoslavs of all races
in the future? What chance of Stanko's little
girl ever managing to put the experiences of

civil war behind her?

That night she decided she ought to ring her husband. She left it till after ten, when she knew he would be back home, and since she preferred to be entirely private she went out into the street and used the nearest phone box.

"Fine," she said, in answer to her husband's first questions. "Lots of fresh sea air, not too many people, food perfectly acceptable. . . . I had a phone call from the children last night."

"Oh dear, I rather thought you might," said Paul, sounding terribly guilty. "Both of them?"

"Yes, they were apparently off to see *Carousel* together. I suspect Mark had mainly gone to London to make sure the new boyfriend, Kevin, is totally acceptable."

"I'm sorry about saying anything to them, but Janet rang, and was curious, and . . ."

"That's perfectly all right. Janet I love and can cope with. I did object, though, to being given good advice by Mark. How did we manage to produce a son with such a plummy voice and such a smug manner?"

"He *has* blotted his copybook! You sound very out of love with him."

"Of *course* I love him. . . . Oh dear, I sound like so many parents I've heard saying *of course* they love their children but they don't actually *like* them very much. Do you think it's possible to love someone without liking them?"

"I'm sure it is. A lot of married couples feel that way about their partners."

"It sounds very uncomfortable. I'm glad I don't feel that way about you."

"That's a lovely thing to say. Thank you." Paul hesitated. "Mark's coming up on Friday."

"Is he? I hope you told him not to bring his washing."

"He's welcome to bring it and do it himself in our machine. . . . I rather think he wants to have a serious talk about you."

"You don't surprise me one little bit."

"Shall I tell him you're working at the problem?"

"No, tell him to get lost. . . . Oh, I am thinking about it on and off, Paul. But I won't have either of you, and especially him, acting as my spiritual physiotherapist. Prescribing spiritual exercises and suchlike."

"Have I?"

"No. But if I hadn't taken a strong line from the beginning you might have."

She finished her phone call as she saw Stanko wandering down the street. She left the phone booth, smiled at him, and together they walked back to the guesthouse.

"I walk about a bit at night," Stanko told her. "Is nice — quiet and nice fresh air. You been phoning someone?"

"My husband. I've been off-loading my irritation at my son. Children — who'd have them?" She saw his face and immediately began apologising. "Oh Stanko — I *am* sorry. How thoughtless of me. I wouldn't for the world . . ."

"Don't you worry, Meesa Rosemary. Don't you think about it again. You have a nice day today?"

And they went upstairs talking naturally and normally, as if, Rosemary thought afterwards, they had known each other for years.

# CHAPTER THREE

# *People Talking*

*I*n the next few days Rosemary settled into a comfortable routine, varied by special treats. The treats included a visit to the theatre (an Ayckbourn, of course) and the first film she had seen in a cinema in years (she found she had simply lost the habit). She visited the art gallery and took some trips out of town by bus, sometimes walking back to the guesthouse.

Otherwise she read, relaxed on the beach or the cliffs, had long afternoon naps if the weather was rainy or windy, and watched some television.

She found she liked to be down in the lounge either for the twenty to six news or the six o'clock one on the BBC. This often meant exposure to Australian soaps in the minutes before. She decided that the appeal of the soaps was that everyone seemed healthy, good-looking and clean — they depicted a sort of hygienic Elysian fields. All the young people had rather nice manners too: she actually saw one ask to get up from table at the end of a meal. Did young people in Australia, she wondered, really ask to get up from table? Did they still sit down at table for meals?

She was watching for news of Bosnia. At home she tended to turn away or turn off, finding the scenes unbearably painful. Now she wanted to know where the fighting was, and who was fighting whom. This was not easy to discover from the television reports. On some days there was no item from what she still thought of as Yugoslavia at all. On others a situation was focussed on, but with hardly any background information, as if knowledge of it was assumed — or perhaps because the reporter had despaired of ever explaining the situation to viewers, or even of understanding it himself. It was like the Schleswig–Holstein dispute: everyone who could explain it was either dead or mad or had forgotten the explanation.

She asked Stanko where the camp was from which he had last heard news of his wife and child. She listened for it, but never heard it mentioned. Finally she bought a pocket atlas and asked him to point out its location to her. Then she listened for mentions of the nearest towns, but when they came they were unilluminating. Some days she bought the *Times* and the *Guardian*, but their reports were mostly about the peace talks in Geneva, and since the only people who seemed to want peace were outside Yugoslavia these seemed futile and doomed. Had the newspapers no longer got reporters where things — horrible things — were actually happening?

"Do you understand what's going on?" she asked Stanko.

"I know *who* is fighting who," he answered gloomily. "I not understand *why.*"

They got into the habit of having little talks together. Rosemary would go down late to dinner, so that by the time she was drinking her coffee she was the only one left in the dining room. Stanko would sit opposite her and together they would swap little tidbits of information about their former lives until the proprietress came in looking disapproving. Sometimes they would meet out walking. Once they found they had the television lounge to themselves in the evening after Stanko had finished work for the day, and there they had a good talk which Rosemary felt she really learnt something from. They were falling into a routine.

41

"I must remember I've got to go home," said Rosemary to herself.

She was reminded of this on the seventh day of her stay by a phone call. It was Sunday, and she had not gone to church, enjoying instead a breezy walk on the North Cliff. She was savouring a better-than-usual pudding when the proprietress, Mrs Blundell, came to tell her there was a phone call for her.

"Probably my husband," said Rosemary, spooning into her mouth the last of the crème brulée and getting up.

"No, it's a . . . woman," said Mrs Blundell. Rosemary knew she had been about to say the word "lady" but had been prevented from doing so by her strict standards of gentility. Rosemary suspected it would be one of Paul's more militant or more gossip-hungry parishioners.

"Rosemary Sheffield," she said cautiously.

"Rosemary, it's Florrie here. Florrie Harridance."

She needn't have given a name. The wheeze and the slow, somewhat threatening delivery identified the caller.

"Oh yes," said Rosemary neutrally. "Hello Florrie."

"Well, we've heard about your problem in the parish, and we're all very sorry," the voice laboured on. "There's a lot of sympathy for you, but there *is* something odd about a clergyman's wife who doesn't believe — there is in my book, any road."

The voice was pure Lancashire, and seemed to spin out the long O in "book" to eternity. Rosemary pictured her at her phone, with her whiskery face, her voracious expression, and her enormous bosom stretching out before her like some kind of personal continental shelf.

"It's certainly not an ideal situation," she said, to say something.

"It certainly is not! Coming at a time when we need a new chair for the Mothers' Union."

Oh yes, thought Rosemary. Now we're getting there.

"Is Mrs Munson really giving up this time?" she asked.

"She is. No question. The arthritis has got her so bad — crippled, she is. Tragic! Oh no, this time she's really going. And of course with you being the vice-chair . . ."

"Oh, I've never regarded myself as Mrs Munson's successor, necessarily," said Rosemary truthfully. "There's many others could do the job. I know Mrs Macauley would like it."

"Hetty Macauley!" This was not at all the name Florrie Harridance wanted to hear, as

Rosemary well knew. "Hetty Macauley hasn't got the energy, she hasn't got the vision, and she hasn't got the common touch. . . ."

Well, if it's the common touch that's needed, you've got it all right, Rosemary thought. She sank gratefully into a chair thoughtfully placed near the reception desk.

"Now you know me, Rosemary: I'm North Country, and I'm blunt with it." Brutal more like, and totally insensitive to others' feelings, Rosemary thought. "I *don't* think it would be suitable for a nonbeliever to take the chairperson's job, and I don't think Hetty Macauley's the person for it either. Now this is going to look like pushing myself forward . . ." It is, Florrie, it is. ". . . but there is a body of opinion in the Mothers' Union that wants me in that job. I'd call it a sort of current of opinion. And since in the present circumstances, if rumour is correct, you couldn't take the job, not in my opinion, then I don't think I'd be doing myself justice if I didn't let my name go forward. And if you found you could support me, nobody would be happier than me. . . ."

And so it went on. Through the wheezy display of Florrie's heavy artillery Rosemary interjected the odd banality, and when the whole business drew towards a close she said briefly that she would think over what Florrie

44

had said and put the phone down without giving her any further chance to draw out the process of self-aggrandisement. She reminded Rosemary of a heavily armed tank advancing into a country where there is no opposition to the invasion.

She sat on in the foyer for a while, thinking over the phone call. So Florrie knew, and was using her knowledge to further her ambitions to take over the Mothers' Union. Others would use the knowledge, doubtless, to further their aims and schemes. Fine by me, Rosemary thought. All the formal positions she held in the parish she had taken on because pressed to or because no one else wanted to take them on. She set much greater store by the more informal aspects of her life as vicar's wife — visiting, helping, cheering.

But she wasn't happy at the knowledge that her present godless state was known to Mrs Harridance. Because if it was known to her that meant it was known to the parish as a whole. The twenty-four hour news service that the BBC has for so long wanted to set up nationally had been anticipated locally by the service provided for St Saviour's and Abbingley generally by Mrs Harridance.

How had she heard? Not from Paul, that was certain. Behind his civilized, concerned

45

facade he was embarrassed and upset by the turn of events. He didn't know how he would cope with the sort of comment that inevitably would follow news leaking out. And if not Paul, who? Rosemary's suspicion immediately fixed on her son. Either Paul had not warned Mark strongly enough or Mark had deliberately gone against parental instructions out of some obscure sense that he knew best how to bring his mother back into the Christian fold. If the latter, he very much mistook his mother's nature. She could not be tricked or badgered back into the faith. Opposition merely aroused her to greater obstinacy. She told herself sadly that children often think they understand their parents but really know nothing about them at all. Perhaps that was because the parents had a life *before* parenthood which remained submerged but waiting to come up once the more arduous duties of being father or mother were over.

Then another thought occurred to her. Florrie had referred to her loss of faith, and had implied that it was generally known. But she'd also said "if rumour is correct." In Florrie's mind rumours went from possibilities to probabilities to facts with the speed of lightning, and in this she did not greatly differ from many other men and women in Paul's congregation. Had her sudden departure from Abbingley sparked off rumours in the parish? She was in no doubt that the rumours would have to be sexual. Rumours were always sexual or financial, and since she had no connection with anything financial beyond managing the tiny bit of money she had inherited, sexual it would have to be. Who might she be thought to be having an affair with?

The only figure who sprang to her mind was Dark Satanic Mills, and as the image of his saturnine good looks, his small-town Clark Gable handsomeness, came to her mind her mouth screwed into a pout of distaste. She would hate her name to be coupled with his. She wondered whether to ring her husband, and her hand had strayed towards the telephone when she thought again. Paul was always the last to hear rumours: even the most eager bearer of ill tidings to the one most affected would be abashed by his patent decency. She'd give it a day or two: by then someone would have summoned up the courage or the effrontery.

In the event, she rang Paul the next evening, Monday night. She was just too curious to know what was being said in the parish to wait any longer. After some friendly preliminaries she said, "How did Mark's visit go?"

"Oh, fine," said her husband, a touch of constraint in his voice. "I didn't see all that much of him because he was around visiting old friends much of the time. But we did, I'm afraid, have a long talk about you. He insisted upon it."

"That boy is becoming a moral steam-roller," said Rosemary, aware of an unmotherly sharpness in her voice. "Couldn't you try to dissuade him from going into the Church?"

"You only say that because you've lost your faith."

"On the contrary: it's the good of the Church I'm thinking about."

"Now you are being unfair."

"No I'm not. It's not clergymen who go off with other men's wives or who collect pornography who do the Church harm — well, it *is*, but more harm is done by pompous prigs like Mark who act as if the Church still had the central part in people's lives that it had in 1850. He thinks he's going to be an important man by going into the Church, poor silly boy. In fact the Church is hardly even marginal any more."

"Well, *I* know that."

"Of course you do. I wish you could get it across to him. . . . Paul?"

"Yes?"

"Did you make clear to Mark that this — this about me — was to be kept under his hat?"

"Ah . . . well, yes I did but . . ."

"Go on."

She could just picture him swallowing and stuttering.

"Well, I got in a bit late. And when I made it clear to him a sort of shifty look came into his eyes."

"I know it well."

"You see, he got here while I was at evensong, and he walked to the Church, and when I came out he was talking to —"

"Florrie Harridance. All right. That explains how she knew. I gather it's all over the parish by now. I rather got the impression there might be other rumours as well."

"If so I haven't heard them. What kind of rumours?"

"Don't know. Maybe that I'm having a mad, passionate affair. Whether this is seen as a reason for or a consequence of my loss of faith I don't know."

"I think you're imagining things. Anyway, you can't blame Mark for *those* rumours."

"He's a blabbermouth. I don't know why he thinks his mother's spiritual state should be the concern of the whole parish."

"Well you *are* a clergyman's wife."

"Don't I know it!"

There was a brief pause.

"Nothing's er . . . ?"

"Happened? No pretty pink cloud of faith has descended? No, Paul, I'm afraid it hasn't. I think that's something we're going to have to live with."

She was being uncharacteristically brutal, and she heard Paul sigh at the other end.

After the phone call she did something unlike her. She left Cliff View, found an off-licence and bought herself a chilled bottle of white wine. She felt oddly embarrassed about it and was glad it was well disguised in an anonymous plastic bag. The phrase "secret drinker" kept coming into her mind. It was still early evening and, once in her room, she poured herself a glass, sat thinking, then sipping, reading a little, and thinking again. Soon after nine she finished *A Tale of Two Cities* and slipped down to the TV lounge to get a replacement. There were three old people in a comatose state watching a sitcom. Wasn't it fun in the old days when we actually *laughed* at the comedy programmes on television, Rosemary thought? There wasn't much joy in the shelf of classics either, but she selected *The Prisoner of Zenda* and took *Adam Bede* just in case the Hope book, which she had never read, proved too awful.

Outside, going up the stairs, she found Stanko, out of his white jacket and black trousers, in the sad and shoddy civvies he wore in the evening. She caught him up.

"Tired?"

"A little. A little bit sad."

"Do you feel like a quick drink? I went out and bought a bottle and I couldn't possibly drink it all."

He smiled the little-boy smile which was his off-duty one and nodded, but put a finger to his lips. At her door he said, "Goodnight, then, Meesa Sheffield," and went to his obscure staircase. Then he came back, treading only on the floorboards he knew did not creak. Rosemary shut the door behind them, not sure whether she felt schoolgirlish or immoral.

"Not approved of?" she asked, fetching a second tooth-mug and speaking quietly.

"I think it would not be," said Stanko carefully. "Is no need to speak quiet. The next rooms is empty."

"You mustn't think I sit here drinking every evening," said Rosemary, pouring. Stanko shrugged. "Well, whether it matters or not, I *don't*. But I felt like it tonight."

"You have problems?"

"No. Well — nothing important like your

problems. I just wanted to think something through."

"And you have?"

"I've thought *about* it. I don't think I've thought it through. It's just a little difficulty, really."

"With your husband to do?"

"With Paul? Oh no. Well, not as you mean it. More to do with his job."

"You told me he was a — a priest. What is your word?"

"Clergyman. Priest sounds too grand, though we do use it in the North."

"So what is your husband's problem?"

"Me. I suddenly . . . lost my faith. Or suddenly realised I didn't have it any more. I really can't describe how or why it happened. But I find I don't believe in God any more."

Stanko leaned forward, his liquid eyes warm and concerned. He looked like a spaniel who has realised his master is in pain.

"Is very sad."

Rosemary hedged.

"Would you be sad if you lost your faith?"

"Of course," he said, surprised. "Is what I . . . *hold*. What I — I have not the word —"

"What you cling to?"

"Yes. Cling to. I lose everything, all I own, all the peoples I love. Is what I cling to."

"Yes, I suppose it would be." In her new mood Rosemary found his words sad and pathetic, where before she would have been moved and admiring. "I hope you will always have it."

"But you do not feel sad?"

She decided to be honest.

"Not at all, I'm afraid," she said briskly. "I sometimes tell myself I will be when my loss sinks in, but so far I haven't felt sad in the least."

"But what is your husband's problem? He has not lost his faith?"

"Oh no. It's not catching. But there will be problems — with his parishioners, and so on."

"What is that word par— ?"

"Parishioners. The people who go to his church."

"Why don't he tell them to mind their own businesses?"

"Good question. I wish he would. But Paul's not like that."

"So what will you do?"

"Go home and face them, I suppose."

"You could pretend."

"I could. On anything else I might, but the thought of pretending to be a Christian rather shocks me. Anyway, from what I hear, my dark secret is out."

"I will miss you when you go."

"I shall miss you, Stanko. I wish you had had news from your family while I was here."

"Sometimes I wish . . ."

"Yes?"

"I wish I had *any* news. Even bad." He looked at her to see how she was reacting. "You understand? That it is almost better to know something terrible has happened than to be . . . like this. Uncertain. Knowing nothing."

Rosemary nodded.

"I understand. My mother said she felt like that during the war, when my father was fighting in North Africa."

"I seem to be living in a dream here," said Stanko, his eyes miles away. "No reality. My wife and little girl they are at war. And I? I serve at table." He stood up. "I go now. You very kind to listen to me. I never met so kind person."

Rosemary had stood up too, worried by his face, which seemed about to crumple. Perhaps to hide it he took her hand and raised it to his lips. She had never had her hand kissed in that Continental way before and hadn't expected Stanko to do it, but as he dropped it she realised that his face was indeed crumpling into tears, and the next thing she knew he was sobbing into her shoulder

— long, anguished, racking sobs, and she could only put her arms round his thin shoulders, murmur words of comfort and encouragement, say she understood, that it was very natural, and all the banalities with which one tries to soothe terrible grief. It occurred to her that she had been in such a situation only with children before. She also wondered where it might end.

It ended with his taking out a grubby handkerchief and dabbing at his eyes.

"You very kind," he said. "I go now."

He was looking straight into her eyes. Rosemary nodded.

"I would like to hear if you get news of your family. I'll give you my address."

"Is not necessary. Is in the book."

"Of course."

"Thank you again. Thank you for so much kindness."

He was at the door now. He looked as if he was going to burst into tears again. Rosemary said firmly, "Good night, Stanko," and he wrenched open the bedroom door and fled out into the corridor. Rosemary heard him running up the stairs to his attic room, but she also heard steps on the main staircase from the ground floor that passed her bedroom and finally went into another room further down the corridor.

She poured herself another large glass of wine and sat in the armchair, thinking hard. This time she thought things through, and came to the conclusion that it was time for her to go home.

## CHAPTER FOUR

# *Homecoming*

*R*osemary fixed her return home for Wednesday. By then she would have been away for ten days, and if anything was going to "happen" (about her loss of faith, of course, not in her relationship with Stanko) it would surely have done so by then. All that had happened, in fact, was that she had shaken down into her agnosticism: it had become more comfortable, like new clothes after a few wearings. The holiday in Scarborough to find herself had in reality been no more than a pleasant break away from home. Now it was time to return to normality.

Things with Stanko had gone no further. He had seemed a little embarrassed by his breakdown in her room, and at breakfast the next day they only exchanged conventional greetings. Rosemary had an uncomfortable feeling, though, that some eyes in the room

57

were fixed on them. At dinner on Tuesday he had dropped a small, square snapshot on to the table, something that looked like a passport photograph. It was a pretty, dark-haired young woman.

"Is my wife," he said.

"She looks very nice," said Rosemary, thinking how staid and middle-class she sounded. But it was quite true: she did look nice. Where was she now, and what had the war done to her?

On Wednesday Rosemary felt no need to hurry home. Paul would be at a Rotarians' dinner that evening, so there was no chance of eating together. She decided to have a last long walk on the beach and then lunch at Cliff View. This was a mistake. When Stanko came to offer her a choice of braised lamb and cod and chips he bent down and hissed in her ear, "Both is offle." She chose the awful cod and chips and settled down to read about the last years of the various Sitwells: eccentricity ripening into sheer awfulness. When, at the end of an extremely boring culinary experience, Stanko brought her coffee he said, "You forgive me for Sunday night?"

"Stanko, there's nothing to forgive."

"Is very not English."

"Sometimes being un-English is a very good thing to be."

"Un-English. Is good word. I learn."

But she felt very English when, as she left, she shook his hand and said, "Keep in touch."

He looked bewildered for a moment, as if her words had something to do with touching her. Then he understood and beamed. "Oh yes, I keep in touch," he said. As she settled her bill she heard him whistling around the kitchen.

She carried her own case again as she walked back to the station, taking a last look at the shops that sold the sort of clothes she wore — she, the wife of a Church of England vicar in a reasonably well-to-do parish, wearing the uniform of her order. The thought still depressed her a little. The train was fairly empty for the first stretch of the way home, but at York she had to change trains, and as she was walking over the bridge she saw ahead of her the figure of one of her husband's parishioners, Selena Meadowes. Rosemary slowed down and looked around her airily, as if seeing the beauties of York station for the first time. But as ill luck would have it, just as Selena was about to board the train she looked around at the station clock and in the process she spotted Rosemary.

"Oh, super!" she said, waving energetically. "Someone to share the journey with."

Without a hint of a query to *her,* Rosemary

thought resentfully, as to whether she wanted her journey shared. But then, clergymen and their wives were generally regarded as always on tap, and not to have needs and preferences of their own.

"Hello Selena," she said in neutral tones. "I wondered if I would see anyone I knew."

Selena breezed ahead, her smile cleaving a way through the bustle of travellers till she found a good double seat facing forward. She was her usual bright, spick-and-span self, all her clothes brightly patterned and sparklingly clean, as if she were dressed for a soap powder ad, and in her usual nice-young-mum style that made the heart sink. She always reminded Rosemary of the heroines in fifties musicals, and she imagined her as anxiously awaiting the return of the dirndl skirt.

"Here we are," she said in her bright soubrette voice. "Golly, you *do* look well, Rosemary. Blooming. Your break away has really done you good."

Probing, thought Rosemary. In fact she was aware that she was being watched very closely.

"Thanks," she said noncommittally.

"So what did you do?"

"Oh, the sort of thing one does at seaside places out of season: walked, read, took in a play. It was an old Ayckbourn — quite funny."

Selena looked as if she was not after drama criticism.

"Well, whatever it is it's certainly agreed with you, I can see that. Did you, er . . ." Here we go, thought Rosemary. "Did you come back any happier?"

"I wasn't suffering from depression, Selena."

Selena looked the tiniest bit embarrassed.

"Oh, I know, but people were saying — Mrs Harridance was saying —"

"Mrs Harridance says a great deal, as you know, and very little of it is to the purpose."

"Oh Rosemary, she means well."

Rosemary raised her eyebrows skeptically.

"When people say that about anyone they usually mean that they blunder about bringing disaster in their wake with the best possible intentions but not an ounce of common sense. I don't see Mrs Harridance like that at all. Florrie Harridance has one thought and one thought only: herself."

Now Selena Meadowes looked shocked. Rosemary had violated a code. One did not make out-and-out condemnations of people if one was a clergyman's wife.

"Rosemary! How unkind of you. You'd never have been so uncharitable . . . before."

"Wouldn't I? I'd have thought it even if I didn't say it, which comes to much the same thing. You were saying that Mrs Harridance said —"

"Well . . . that you were having . . . *problems*. Spiritual problems."

"You could call it that. I lost my faith."

Selena looked terribly concerned, as if she had said that her puppy had disappeared.

"And the break away didn't . . . change anything?"

"No. I never really thought it would. What is that saying about travellers changing the sky above them but not themselves? I don't see why anyone should expect to find God in Scarborough, in any case."

"You must be *awfully* unhappy," said Selena soulfully. Since she had just been trying to convey exactly the opposite, Rosemary was annoyed.

"Not at all. I'm perfectly happy."

"But your whole life was centred on your belief in God."

"Was it? I think you must have been under an illusion about me, Selena. It had become not much more than a routine. Now it's gone it's as if a blanket has been lifted from over my head. Now I can breathe properly at last."

"Oh Rosemary!"

"It's as well to speak the truth, isn't it?

That is precisely how I feel."

"But what will you *do?*"

"Do? I don't see that I'm called on to do anything."

"But . . . maybe I shouldn't say anything."

"Do. I'm quite unshockable."

"Mrs Harridance feels you shouldn't play any part in parish affairs as long as you're an unbeliever."

Rosemary smiled grimly. "Back to Victorian values, eh? Ostracise the unbeliever. Well, that will give me a lot of spare time, which will be very welcome. I wonder what I should do with it? Take up macramé, perhaps, or study for an Open University degree. I wonder what Mrs Harridance would advise."

"I'm not saying everyone agrees with her, of course."

"I should hope not," said Rosemary, in tones that were becoming positively grim. "I should be sorry to think that the spirit of Mrs Harridance had infected the whole parish."

"You *are* unfair to her, Rosemary."

"Could we talk about something else, Selena? I'll have quite enough talk about this when I get home to Paul."

"Oh, I am sorry!" Selena's face was quite guileless, which showed what faces could do.

"I thought you'd *want* to talk about it. I know I would."

"Well, I don't. And please tell anyone who asks that I don't. Has anything else happened while I've been away?"

"I don't think so, Rosemary. Stephen Mills has agreed to talk to the Mothers' Union on 'Business Ethics and the Christian Religion.'"

"What would he know about either?"

"Rosemary! You *are* changed."

Rosemary kept up her brisk, unkindly tone, which she found very palate-cleansing.

"Now don't pretend you don't know there are lots of people in the parish who are extremely suspicious about Mr Mills."

"Well, I think they're very unfair. You shouldn't be suspicious unless you've got good, concrete reasons. . . . And he's so dishy!"

"Do you think so?"

"Well, you can't deny *that*. Film-star looks. When he looks me straight in the eye I go positively weak at the knees."

"I have a physical reaction, certainly, but not that one."

"Don't tell anyone, will you?" Selena was not listening to anything said to her and gave a tiny giggle. "Me, a happily married woman!"

"Your secret is safe with me. I'm just glad

you're not one of those whose knees go to jelly at the sight of Paul. I don't know what it is about a clergyman that *gets* to some women."

"Your husband is *awfully* attractive for his age."

"I'll tell him you said so. He'll be terribly grateful. Now I think about it, maybe you'd better keep quiet about some of the things I've said today. I don't want to cause him more trouble than he'll have from me anyway."

"Of course, Rosemary! Silent as the grave."

On the way home on the bus Rosemary wondered why she had bothered attempting to ensure Selena's silence. She belonged to the Florrie Harridance Broadcasting Corporation, and everything Rosemary had said would be round the parish by the next day. By the time she had settled herself comfortably in at home, deciding that it really was nice to be back among familiar things again, she was starting to ask herself why she had said anything to Selena Meadowes at all. She knew what she was like, she had no liking for her, yet she had blabbed to her as if she was discretion itself. Had she got some kind of parochial death wish? Did she see her work with Paul in Abbingley as at an end? If so, Paul ought to have been the first to be told.

And when she really got down to hard thinking, she was not at all sure that this was
what she wanted.

Paul was in and out quickly at six, kissing
her warmly and saying it was wonderful to
have her home, then changing into black tie
and decrepit dinner jacket and going out looking infinitely seedier than he would have in
a lounge suit or clericals. Rosemary listened
to a Nielsen symphony, watched the ten
o'clock news with her usual hunger for reports from Yugoslavia, and waited for his return. When she heard the car pull into the
garage it was clear he had someone with him.

"It's just Stephen," Paul called as he came
through the front door. "Come to get the
Rotary Club books."

He bustled in and went to his study and
over to the bookcase, where the account
books had been piled in readiness. Dark Satanic Mills came in to the hall and stood in
the living room doorway with his usual
smooth confidence.

"Hello Rosemary," he said. "Welcome
back."

He did look handsome, Rosemary thought,
against the half-light from the hall. In fact,
he stood there posing as handsome, exuding
the confidence of handsomeness, *broadcasting*
his handsomeness. He was not tall, in fact

66

he was almost stocky, but he had shiny black hair, each strand immaculately in place, and perfect features set in a sallow skin. Women notice me, his bearing announced. And if they have anything I want, I notice them.

"Hello Stephen," Rosemary said.

"Here they all are," said Paul, coming through and handing over a small pile of heavy books. "I couldn't be happier about handing them over. You'll make a much better job of it than I could ever do."

"Nonsense, you've done a wonderful job," said Stephen Mills, hardly bothering to put conviction in his voice. "Now, I'll make myself scarce. You two will have a lot to talk about, and I'll only be intruding if I stay for coffee."

Which you have not been offered, Rosemary thought, and your mentioning it is your way of drawing attention to the omission. When Paul came in from showing him out she said:

"The church mouse handing over to the church rat."

"The Rotary Club has nothing to do with the Church," said Paul pedantically. "I will admit that Stephen would not have been my first choice as treasurer, but h—"

"But he offered. Of course he did."

"Don't make too much of it. I don't think

for a moment he'll do anything improper."

"Nor do I. Too many shrewd financial brains among the Rotarians. But he'll milk the job for all it's worth as far as contacts and mutual favours are concerned."

"True. But enough of Dark Satanic."

"More than."

"Is it good to be home? Would you like a nightcap?"

"It's lovely! Do you mean an alcoholic one?" Paul nodded. "Is there any red wine open?"

"There is. I cooked for myself last night and compensated for the awfulness of it with a glass or two." He went to the kitchen and came back with a half-full bottle. As he was pouring her a glass he said casually, "Situation still as it was?"

"Oh yes. I don't think there's much point in talking about that, Paul, if you don't mind. It is as it is, and if it changes it does, but it won't be through anything we've done. . . . I met Selena Meadowes on the train from York."

"Brightly sparkling as ever?"

"At least."

"Did she say something that worried you?"

"Isn't marriage dreadful?" said Rosemary, sipping her wine. "Each partner is the nearest thing to a thought policeman there is. . . .

Not worried, exactly, but she did make me think. Apparently Florrie Harridance is spreading it around that since I'm now an unbeliever I shouldn't play any part in parish affairs or any of the groups and activities."

"I'm sure Selena has got it wrong."

"I don't think so."

"Florrie's a very silly woman if she's saying that kind of thing. People don't take kindly to witch hunts these days."

Rosemary thought that over seriously.

"*Most* people. . . . And actually I'm not even sure that that is true. Witch hunts are what the tabloid press is based on."

"St Saviour's isn't a tabloid parish."

"Don't you believe it! The *Sunday Times* delivered, and the *People* bought surreptitiously while walking the dog. Anyway, the *Sunday Times* is just a tabloid for the upper-middle classes."

"Would it worry you, taking a back seat?"

"I think what she wants is to push me out of the car. No, not at all. Or not much. I'd been thinking anyway about what I might do, and I was coming to the conclusion that the Open University was made for people like me, whose children have left home. But something in me really dislikes being pushed."

"Good for you."

"And I don't like the thought of the spirit of Florrie Harridance taking over the parish either."

"Don't make a bogey-woman of her, Rosemary."

"I don't need to. She's done that herself."

Paul swerved from the subject.

"So you'll fight. I think that's excellent. You'll try and stay on as vice-chair of the Mothers' Union."

"It's not just offices like that. I'm not mad about the Mothers' Union. They always remind me of a line in a song we used to sing at school: 'They laugh, and are glad, and are *terrible*.' But I am going to resist her, generally. I am going to try to get across what a mean, restrictive, vengeful sort of attitude hers is. Not to say self-promotional."

"Good for you."

"I'm not sure *how* I'm going to fight her. It will be difficult to oppose her without saying precisely what I think of her, which would make things difficult for you."

"Turning the other cheek is excellent advice, you know."

Rosemary smiled at him. He didn't give up.

"You'd have to say that," she said.

"No, I mean it. If you prefer to put it in worldly terms, it's a wonderful *ploy*. It puts the other person so wonderfully in the wrong and gets sympathy immediately on to your side."

"How Machiavellian of you, Paul. I've never thought of you as that before. You may be right, but turning the other cheek is not something Christians often do, is it? I've never seen such a bellicose lot, in general, or such dirty fighters."

"It's not unusual, is it, for people not to live up to their religion? It happens in all of the faiths. Christians haven't realised yet that returning good for evil, as well as being right, is an extremely clever move. If you stay meek and mild while Florrie Harridance gets more and more dogmatic and extreme, you'll soon have everyone on your side."

"It's a thought," said Rosemary. "I'll consider it."

But she didn't tell Paul that, if turning the other cheek was to be her strategy, she had made a very bad start on the train that day.

# CHAPTER FIVE

# *The Other Cheek*

*R*osemary had always seen it as her job as vicar's wife to provide a practical backup to her husband's ministry. Paul went round to see the sick and the dying, providing them with spiritual comfort and a shoulder to cry on. Rosemary dropped in on the same people to make sure they had home helps, meals on wheels and plenty of reading matter. The young mothers mostly ran their own groups in the church hall or the vestry, but Rosemary went along to them now and then and was always in the background willing to give advice when problems arose. They seldom did, because the young mothers were too busy for the rumour-mongering and backbiting that the older members of the congregation went in for. Thus, her role was practical, and she tried to avoid involvement with any of the parish groups or diocesan bodies. Those were the sorts of activity she found boring and shouldered with reluctance.

Nevertheless she was vice-chair of the local Mothers' Union branch, and she was on the various committees that arranged such parish events as the harvest festival, fêtes and bring-and-buy sales. They were positions she would have relinquished very readily if it had not been Florrie Harridance who was trying to shoulder her off. She kept in the forefront of her mind a mental picture of Florrie, with her bustle, her bulk and her endless steam-kettle monologue, as she went about her business as Paul's pastoral adjunct.

She called next morning on Violet Gumbold, a Mothers' Union stalwart, though her children, like Rosemary's, were grown up and had moved away. Mrs Gumbold had broken her leg on the day Rosemary went to Scarborough, and as her husband was a commercial traveller and away much of the time, she needed all the help from the parish that she could get.

Rosemary took away a list of shopping basics Violet needed and three library books to change, repressing the feeling that Stephen King and Robert B. Parker were not the sick-bed reading she would have chosen. When she came back Violet Gumbold had hobbled round to make tea and biscuits. Together they sat down comfortably over them.

"Did you enjoy Scarborough?" Rosemary was asked.

"Yes, I did. Lots of fresh, clean air and good walks."

"They say you're going through a sort of . . . crisis."

"You could say that. Do you mind if we don't talk about it, Violet? I seem to have done nothing but talk it over with Paul and others in the family."

"I'm sorry, Rosemary. I should have thought. Will this make any . . . any difference?"

"I really don't know. If people want me to *withdraw*, then there are plenty of things I could do."

"Oh no, Rosemary, nobody wants *that*." Rosemary waited for her to say what they did want, and Violet began to flounder and go rather red. "You do the parish work so wonderfully well we couldn't possibly manage without you. We'd all be at sea. . . . Mrs Harridance came round the other day."

"That was nice of her, to come and help," said Rosemary, meekly and maliciously.

"She didn't actually h— . Well, but while she was here she said she thought, since you had lost your faith, maybe you shouldn't stay on as vice-chair in the Mothers' Union, and the way she put it it did seem . . ."

Mrs Gumbold's attitude appeared to be akin to saying it was all right for her to muck out the stables so long as she didn't try to ride the horses. She was not the strongest brain in the parish, though Rosemary had always found her well-meaning. She just said, "I'll leave that entirely up to the members. I wouldn't dream of staying on if that wasn't what they wanted."

Mrs Gumbold looked relieved, as if she had in some way done her duty, or done what she had been told.

"Oh well — that's all right then. I'm sure . . . Mrs Harridance was talking about the chairmanship as well."

"Of the Mothers' Union? Yes, she rang me about that."

"I believe Mrs Munson is adamant that this time she *will* go."

"She's done a wonderful job over the years. I'm sure everyone will understand."

"And if it goes by hard work then Mrs Harridance has worked like a Trojan too, and you could say . . ."

She faded into silence and looked at Rosemary. Once again Rosemary had the sense that she had said what she had been told to say. She also had the feeling that Violet Gumbold didn't actually like Mrs Harridance any more than she did.

"We're so lucky in the Mothers' Union, aren't we?" Rosemary said brightly, feeling herself an awful hypocrite. "There's so many who are willing to work hard for us. There's Mrs Macauley, and there's Mrs Bannerman, who can never do enough, and —"

"Oh, do you think Mrs Bannerman could be the chairwoman of the Mothers' Union? That would be nice — she's such a pleasant person, and very efficient." Mrs Gumbold frowned, uncertainly. "But she's not an educated woman."

"I don't see what that's got to do with it," Rosemary said briskly. "What we need is someone hard-working and capable, and she certainly is that. So is Mrs Harridance, of *course*, but she's hardly an educated person either."

"No. . . . Do have another biscuit, Rosemary."

That conversation was the first of several Rosemary was to have over the next few days. She never brought up the subject of her loss of faith or her position in the parish, but when it came up she always expressed herself quite happy to abide by the views of the majority. She suspected that her apparent determination not to put up a fight meant that many resolved to put up a fight for her. She became quite certain Mrs Harridance wanted her off the committee because she knew her opinion of her. She accordingly never wavered from her expressed belief that Mrs Harridance would make an *excellent* chairwoman, and that they were lucky to have so many hard workers who would all do a splendid job if they were to think of putting up for the chairwoman's position.

"I do think a real election is often a good idea," said Mrs Munson, the retiring chair. "Rather than its just going to someone by default."

"It does clear the air," Rosemary agreed.

Such conversations were always conducted with the utmost meekness (which was a bit of a strain). They did seem to Rosemary after a time to be bearing fruit. Her antennae were keenly attuned to the niceties of parish opinion, she having been among these people for the last twelve years, and when she saw people talking together in muted tones she could tell from their stance and the way they looked at her whether they were on her side or against her. She rather thought that by and large they were on her side. It occurred to her that Mrs Harridance, for all her appearance of steamrolling forward and never hearing a word anyone else said, also had antennae that were at least sensitive enough to get the same message. If they were, she suspected that she might be getting a social call from her.

It came when she had been home a little more than a week. She saw Florrie approaching from the direction of the park, her ample figure wrapped in a bright blue coat, with a large, flowery hat covering her tight curls. Her somewhat protuberant eyes had the glint of purpose in them, but then they always did. Florrie had something of the purposive air of an outsize rodent.

Rosemary did not rush down to let her in, but waited till she heard the doorbell, then walked down to her visitor in a leisurely fashion.

"Rosemary, you do look well."

"Thank you, Florrie."

"People have been saying you did, but we don't run into each other like we used to, with you not coming to church."

"No, we don't," said Rosemary neutrally.

"It's a pity, that. Means you're bound to be a bit out of touch."

She had taken off her hat and come through to the living room, where she sat down determinedly on the sofa. Rosemary did not offer her coffee or tea because Florrie always refused them (they interfered with her monologues). Rosemary sat opposite her in the big armchair, wondering which cheek was the other one that she ought to turn.

"Because naturally we've all been thinking about you and your position, Rosemary — in a Christian spirit, of course . . ." She stared at Rosemary, as if daring her to object, or to laugh. "Because of course we all hope you'll be back with us *fully* before long, I mean in *spirit* as well, but really what we do feel is that the Mothers' Union is a *church* group, a *Christian* group. So we understand your still wanting to be part of it, but on the other hand . . ."

Rosemary sat back and let it roll over her. It wasn't pleasant, but these days one's ear was used to unrelenting noise: one had only to go into the centre of Leeds to be assaulted by sounds of diggers, demolition trucks, high-speed drills and chain saws, and every pub she knew had music in various degrees of loudness in the background. Florrie in a small room produced much the same effect as the drills and the chain saws. Sometimes Rosemary made an effort to check her flow, but on this occasion she knew that eventually Florrie was going to have to get to a question that demanded from her an answer. After ten minutes or so it came.

"Now, what I'm sure would be best, Rosemary dear, would be if you resigned now as vice-chair, just went quietly. Everyone will understand, and there certainly won't be any criticism, and that way there won't be any nastiness, and I'm sure that for Paul's sake — who we all respect so much — that's what you'd want to avoid."

Rosemary wanted to object that bringing Paul into it like that was fighting dirty, but she kept the other cheek resolutely turned. The monologue went on a bit longer, but eventually Florrie had to draw to a close and look interrogatively at Rosemary.

"I'm just going to leave it to the members," she said.

There was a silence of several seconds. Florrie glared, then smiled forgivingly.

"I don't think you've been following, Rosemary dear. What we felt was there'll be so much less nastiness if you —"

"There's been no nastiness, Florrie. You've all been very nice about it. So there'll be no need for any in the future. I'll just go to the next full meeting, tell them the problem (though of course everyone knows by now) and then leave the meeting and they can take the decision."

"Oh Rosemary dear that is *awfully* unwise. Because if you were quietly to resign now saying it's because after all it is a *church* organisation and you'd feel out of place *now*, you wouldn't get the same feeling of rejection as you will if —"

"I'm sorry, Florrie. I won't feel rejected at all. I've made up my mind. I'm afraid I have to go now. I've said I'd go and do some shopping for Mrs Gumbold. I believe you've been helping her since she's been laid up. She told me about your visit. So kind. She needs everyone rallying around now . . ."

And she ushered her to the front door, through it and out to the gate, leaving her time for only a few parting shots.

"I *wish* you would think again Rosemary, because we've all got your interests at heart and —"

Rosemary was just turning to go in again when she realised that a BMW had pulled up in the road opposite, on the park side, its windows down. Dark Satanic Mills got out and lounged over the road, a smile playing on the corners of his lips.

"Good for you, Rosemary. I like a woman who fights."

He didn't say it sexily, but somehow there was sex in the background.

"Good morning, Stephen. What can I do for you?"

He left a pause, to suggest that there was a variety of things he could think of. That was the trouble with overtly sexy people: almost anything one said seemed capable of a second meaning when one talked with them.

"I think Paul has missed out on one of the account books for the Rotarians," he said easily. "Not important, but I need it to get the whole picture. I should think it will be in his study. Any chance of my coming in to have a look for it?"

Rosemary led the way in, and then watched him as he rummaged around for it. As she was watching she considered her reactions to him. Of course the "Satanic" epithet was absurd. No one imagined him indulging in devil-worshipping rituals with children, or dipping his hands into disembowelled animals or birds. Still, the word somehow did seem to fit him: there hovered over him the *possibility* of evil. In fact, Rosemary could imagine all sorts of nastinesses, shading off into outright evil, and could fit them in with his character. And yet, as Paul said, he had been a regular churchgoer in the parish for well over a decade now.

Why did he come? There was not the slightest suspicion of anything spiritual about him. Yet on consideration Rosemary would have had to admit that the same was true of quite a number of the St Saviour's regulars. Yet about Dark Satanic Mills there hung an air of earthiness, greed, sensuality and a total lack of scruple, and *that* was not something that could be said of the other less-than-spiritual communicants. He's not at all *churchy,* she said to herself. He's amoral, outside any code of ethics, totally self-absorbed. Perhaps in the nineteenth century such a man would go along to church to establish some kind of credentials, leading enthusiastically a second life of sin and corruption. But at the latter end of the twentieth century? Today nobody could be *bothered* with that sort of hypocrisy. So why was Mills?

"There it is," said Stephen Mills, making a quick dart and taking a heavy ledger from among books of theology and paperbacks of popular devotion. "What an odd shelving system your husband has."

"It's all his own," agreed Rosemary, waiting for him to go. He stood there, clutching the book to his chest, smiling at her — *knowing* she was wanting him gone.

"So what are the old biddies on about?" he asked.

Rosemary played for time, unwilling to discuss her personal position with him.

"Mrs Harridance wouldn't thank you for calling her an old biddy. She's a woman in the prime of life."

"You haven't answered my question."

"I don't think I need to, Stephen. You always have your finger on the pulse of the parish."

He smiled, almost purred, in self-satisfaction.

"So it's your sudden godlessness, is it? I guessed as much. What do they want? For you to parade down the Ilkley Road in penitential sackcloth?"

"They want — Mrs Harridance wants — me to give up any parish positions I hold."

"And you?"

"I'm just leaving it up to the members."

"Isn't that good enough for her?"

"No. Because she's afraid they'll support me. She wants me to resign quietly so there's no contest."

"Why?"

"Because she wants to be chairwoman of the Mothers' Union, and she wants one of her cronies as deputy, not someone who knows her for what she is — on the make."

She regretted saying that as soon as it was out of her mouth. What *was* it about Dark Satanic Mills, that he could screw things out of you even as you felt distrustful and repelled? And what else was Mills himself but on the make?

"What is there in these jobs?" asked Mills, seemingly genuinely curious. "What's in it for them?"

"Nothing in your sense," said Rosemary. "Nothing in the way of money or contacts or suchlike. But position, prestige, something to bustle about, be self-important about."

Mills had nodded when she talked about money and contacts, the little smile playing around his lips as she showed him how she viewed him — which was probably why he had asked the question in that form in the first place. As usual, he'd got what he wanted. Now he started for the door.

"Very odd, that's what I say. Well, I must be on my way. Tell Paul I've collected this, will you, Rosemary? And —" he put his face close to hers — "go on fighting back. Show them what you're made of."

But over the next week Rosemary found very little call for fighting or for showing what she was made of. If anybody brought up the matter of her loss of faith she repeated the formula of "leaving it up to the members" of any organisation she was involved with to decide whether it made any difference. But very few people brought it up. It was increasingly accepted: it had happened, it was nobody's fault, and Rosemary was just the same person she had always been. It had been a nine days' wonder, and the nine days were over. Rosemary could imagine that when she brought the matter before the Mothers' Union committee the members' main reaction would be to wonder why she had raised it at all.

She was told by a friend that Florrie Harridance had tried to get a local *Yorkshire Post* reporter interested in the matter as a news story. But in the reporter's view it had not had the human interest to compete with the declining fortunes of Leeds United or the total hopelessness of the Yorkshire cricket team. It lacked sex, passion or fanaticism, and news stories involving clergy and their families had to have at least one of those. The reporter had shaken his head and gone on his way.

Rosemary went about her parish work as usual, but she no longer went to church on a Sunday. This meant that she saw much less of Florrie Harridance and her cronies. She did bump into Selena Meadowes one day in the library, and they fell into their usual topic of conversation, the needs of several elderly members of the congregation. For once, though, Selena gave the conversation a personal twist.

"You can't tell me anything about the decline of the elderly," she said, still in her bright tone which seemed so inappropriate. "My poor old Mum seems to have less and less interest in life every time I see her or call her."

"I didn't know you had elderly parents, Selena."

"One, just the one: my mother."

"You must have been a late child."

"I was. What can you do, Rosemary, if they just seem not to want to go on living any more?"

"I don't know. My mother's still very lively. Isn't she interested in the grandchildren?"

"Not very. Oh — I'm being unfair. She likes to *see* them, but then quite soon she's had enough and wishes they'd go away. I wonder whether I shouldn't try a change of scene for her."

"Where does she live?"

"Near Skipton. She used to go to Morecambe for her holidays when my father was alive, but she says she wouldn't want to go back, with all the changes, and from what I hear it's a depressing place now. I wondered whether to try to get her to Scarborough."

"Well, I certainly enjoyed it. But it might be less attractive for someone who's less active. All those hills."

"Where did you stay?"

"It's a place called Cliff View. On St Nicholas's Cliff, near where Anne Brontë died."

Selena Meadowes bridled a little.

"That's literary, isn't it? We're not a very literary family, I'm afraid. Is the food good — traditional, I mean? She's very conservative."

"Yes — anyhow it's perfectly decent."

"I think I might try taking her myself. Then she might stay a fortnight, if I got her really settled in, and I could go and fetch her and take her home."

They smiled and parted then, and the conversation passed from Rosemary's mind as she went about her usual duties, which did not get any less onerous. It was over a week later, when Selena Meadowes's name came up in conversation with Paul over dinner, that Rosemary said:

"I didn't realize she had an elderly mother, going towards senility."

"Really?" Paul said, looking up. "That is sad. I met her once, a year or two ago. Perfectly spry and interested in everything — I wouldn't have said she was more than sixty."

Rosemary knew, from more than one case in the parish, how sadly early Alzheimer's disease could strike. It was a horrific stalking-horse, a terror more actual to most than AIDS. She said no more, but the subject of Selena's mother — or, more particularly,

Selena's motives — remained in the back of her mind.

She rang her own mother that evening, while Paul was out at a Parochial Church Council meeting. Her mother was a lively old lady living in Lincoln, very much taken up with clerical controversies and quarrels, of which there were an inordinate number in Lincoln. Rosemary had been keeping her loss of faith from her, but thinking of Selena Meadowes's mother made her decide that this was the sort of misplaced consideration that the old could do without — that it was, in fact, positively insulting. Her mother took the revelation in her stride, was almost dismissive.

"Probably your time of life," she said. "It will pass. It's probably due to your having *so much* to do with Christians. They can be very depressing, you know. How are the children?"

The question made Rosemary think how much more sensibly her mother had reacted than her son. There was a lot to be said for experience — she hoped Mark would be able to learn from it when it came to him. She was just telling her mother about her son, and trying to keep her irritation with him out of her voice, when the front doorbell rang.

"Must go, Mother. Someone at the door."

It was half past nine — late for a parishioner to visit. She put down the receiver, hurried to the door and put on the front light. Not a shape she recognised. But she had no apprehensions and opened the door. It was Stanko, an appealing, apologetic smile on his face.

"Rosemary, can you help me please? I am in much trouble."

# CHAPTER SIX

# *Place of Safety*

*R*osemary drew Stanko inside and led him through to the living room. She looked at him in the better light there.

"You look tired," she said, "and hungry."

"A little," said Stanko. "I was told I must go middle morning. I went to do packing —" he gestured towards a pathetically small and ill-filled knapsack — "and then I said good-bye and went to coach station. Coach is cheaper, you see. When we get to Leeds I have great difficulty finding bus to Abbingley — everybody very kind and try to help but I go wrong."

"Well, sit down. I'll get you a hot drink, and then I'll make you an omelette or something."

Rosemary found she rather enjoyed fussing over Stanko, as he had fussed over her in the dining room at Cliff View. She lit the gas fire because the evening was getting chilly, made him a pot of coffee, then made a big mushroom omelette with a salad and opened some tins to make some kind of sweet. She was just sitting down opposite him and saying, "Now," when she heard Paul's key in the door. She smiled at Stanko encouragingly, said "Don't worry" and slipped out into the hall.

"We have a visitor," she said.

An unexpected visitor was not an unusual occurrence in a vicar's life. Paul nodded and waited.

"It's the waiter at the guesthouse in Scarborough — I told you about him."

"Good Lord, the Yugoslav boy? What's he doing here?"

"He says he's in trouble."

Paul nodded again, and went in and introduced himself. Rosemary felt herself blessed in having so unflappable and unsuspicious a husband. Stanko was looking less drawn and lean now, and she thought Paul was liking him already.

"Well, what's the trouble, then, Stanko?" Paul asked, when they had all sat down.

Stanko put the bowl with fruit and cream in it down on the table in front of him and sat with his hands in his lap.

"I get the sack," he said.

"Is that so terrible?" asked Paul. "Surely

there must be lots of jobs in seaside places at the moment, with the summer season coming up."

Stanko nodded.

"Is true. But Mrs Blundell she say the police is getting very strict. Always before I have — what do you say? — been a jump in front of them." He gave Paul a shy, conspiratorial glance from lowered eyes. "You see, I have always heard when they have started to make enquiries — in Whitby, at Robin Hood Bay and so on — so I get out before they come. But Mrs Blundell says they are making a . . . a *drive* she calls it, in all the seaside towns, in the smaller restaurants and hotels."

Paul had not stiffened up his easy stance in his chair.

"What you're saying is you've no work permit."

"No. I got passport, but I not got work permit."

There was silence in the room for a moment. Neither Stanko nor Rosemary was looking at Paul, but Rosemary's heart was in her mouth, wondering what he was going to say next.

"I wish we had more contacts in the hotel or restaurant trade."

Rosemary blamed herself for doubting him.

Of course he would take the humane decision. He always had in the past. It could only have been a slight twinge of guilt on her part that had made her doubt he would this time.

"There's no one in the congregation that springs to mind," she said, keeping the relief out of her voice.

"It's something we'd better think about tomorrow," said Paul, who could take snap decisions when necessary but tried to avoid them. "There's no problem about a bed, is there?"

"No — Mark's is still made up from his visit while I was away. If you can put up with it tonight I can change it tomorrow, Stanko."

"No, no — you go to no trouble. Is fine."

"I think," said Paul slowly, "it will be best if you lie fairly low while you're here. A clergyman is not exactly in the public eye, but he is observed by his congregation. Someone they don't know — and an obvious foreigner, as you are — coming to see me would cause no comment, but someone coming and going and obviously living here might."

"That's true," said Rosemary, who knew all too well parish habits of mind. "What we really need to find is a job with some kind of living accommodation thrown in."

"A room, a shared room — anything!" said

Stanko. "If the police catch me they send me straight back to Gorazde — anyway to Bosnia. Back to fighting and being bombed. You understand, Rosemary, I *can't* go back there. I'd rather die!"

Paul touched his arm.

"Yes, we *do* understand, both of us. We'll do what we can, but we need to think carefully first. You really do think the police in Leeds are likely to be less active in hunting down illegal immigrants than those on the coast?"

Stanko nodded quickly. He had obviously thought about it.

"I think so. I hope so. Is in London and the seaside towns we mostly work, and in London is only in the small, not very nice hotels. I think they will not look very hard in Leeds."

"You have contacts with others?"

He nodded hesitantly.

"With a few. Is my countrymen, you understand? They speak my language."

"Of course, of course. Now — I think it's time for bed for you, my lad."

Rosemary noticed that Paul's tone had become fatherly — and fatherly as if towards quite a young child. Yet he knew Stanko was married with a child of his own. Somehow his reaction was not unlike her own to

Stanko's air of well-meaning bewilderment.

In bed later on Paul said, "you know, I've been thinking, and I think the personal touch is called for here. I think we should go to Gianni's for lunch."

Rosemary frowned.

"I suppose it's the best we can do. Gianni is a dear, of course, but we can hardly pretend that we're regular customers."

"Gianni gives me a little of the respect he would give to one of his own priests," said Paul, amusement in his voice. "I don't expect him to offer the boy a job, but he could wise us up on the best avenues of approach."

"That's true. I'll give Stanko the run of the cupboards and the deep freeze for his lunch and we'll go out. It seems ages since we had lunch out together."

"You think I was right about his lying low while he's here?"

"Very much so. There are eyes watching us — cat's eyes."

"It's sad for the lad to be cooped up."

"Oh rubbish, Paul: Think what he'd be if he was in Sarajevo or Gorazde. And he knows that, poor man, only too well. . . . Oh, and thanks, Paul."

He looked at her in astonishment.

"You didn't think there was any question of my handing him over or showing him the door, I hope, Rosemary?"

"No," she said, not entirely truthfully. "But I'm just saying 'thank you' to *some*body, *some*thing, for having married me to a man who wouldn't consider doing that."

The next day they went to Gianni's late on, leaving behind a Stanko who looked much better — less hungry, more relaxed — and was anxious to be useful around the house. They suggested it was best if he didn't answer the door or the telephone. Gianni's was an unpretentious but warm and inviting trattoria off the Ilkley Road. It was moderately full with lunchtime eaters when they arrived at one fifteen, to a genial but respectful welcome from Gianni himself. By the time they had had their soup and pasta it was two o'clock, and most of the customers had disappeared back to work.

"You not like something else? Ice-cream? Zabaglione? Coffee?" Gianni enquired.

"Two coffees, please — cappuccino," said Paul. "And we would like a word with you if you have a moment." Gianni nodded, apparently pleased and flattered, and five minutes later he came back with the coffee and sat himself at their table.

"How can I 'elp? You want to come over to the Cat'olics, like a lot of your priests and politicians?"

"Not this week, maybe next," said Paul. They all chuckled. Gianni was a genuinely devout Catholic.

"Woman priests! What an atrocity!" He saw a look in Rosemary's eyes, and quickly said, "But we don't quarrel, eh?"

"I'm sure we won't," said Paul, ever the conciliator. "I'm sad about the priests, but you're welcome to the politicians. What we want is advice. We want to know —" he looked around him and lowered his voice — "how to go about finding a job in the catering or hotel trade for someone who . . . who doesn't have all the necessary paper work."

Gianni shot him a quick, suspicious glance, but seemed reassured by the clerical collar which Paul had taken care to wear. It was a useful piece of superstition and seemed to work even though Paul had his wife with him.

"Forgive me. One 'as to be careful."

"Of course. We're trying to be."

"Not that I myself —" Gianni leaned back expansively in his chair, once again the genial host — "not that I myself would need to employ such a person. A business which is doing very nicely does not need to — *capisce?*" He exuded proprietorial satisfaction. "But I tell you this: when the recession was at its worstest, I think of it, eh? I consider. Because

98

then it was all 'cut this cost, cut that cost,' otherwise —" he brought his hand down like a guillotine on to the table.

"We thought you might know *something* about it, even though not from experience," explained Rosemary guilefully. "You're the only person in the trade we really know."

Gianni paused to say farewell to a departing party of regulars. Now they were the only people in that part of the restaurant.

"You have a person in this country, and you want to find him a job — maybe a place to stay, a room over?"

"That's right. That would be ideal."

"You not want to talk to your Mr Mills?"

"Stephen Mills?" said Rosemary sharply. "Why would we want to talk to him? Stephen doesn't have anything to do with the restaurant trade."

"No, no. But he is a good — how do you say? — organiser. He know how to get things done."

"He's a fixer," said Rosemary.

"Exactly! A feexer!"

"I would *very* much rather not bring in Stephen Mills," Rosemary said.

"Right. I understand." He looked amused and smiled slyly. "Is a man who the ladies like very much or not at all. Maybe not at all is wisest. So, you do it yourselves, eh?

Now let us talk turkey, like you say. Hotels in Leeds, they are not like seaside hotels. In Leeds there is not a hundred and one little guesthouses that are very difficult to investigate. On the other 'and, little takeaway food places —"

"Pizza takeaways?"

"*Esattamente!* 'Pizza and Pasta,' 'Pizza Pronto' — that kind of thing. They are all over the place. Some is family establishments — the big family, you understand, with distant cousins brought over from Sicily to learn the trade and learn the language, though mostly they don' learn the trade and they don' learn the language. Is not suitable, such places. But other places, where there is one man, who has seen an opportunity, an opening you say, where there is perhaps an area with many many students and no takeaway — such a man with no large family behind him . . ."

"That sounds just the job," said Paul.

"Your man — he can make pizzas?"

"I'm sure he can," said Rosemary firmly.

"Is silly to ask. Anyone can make pizzas, pizzas that students will eat. They just want to be filled up, as cheap as possible because they're living on loans. Now, I give you four names, just to start with." He wrote rapidly on the back of their bill. "You try Signor

Gabrielli first. Is a very nice man, good Cat'olic, but not very wealthy. Struggling a little bit, you know? He try to help if he can. Ring him up maybe eight, half past eight. When the early evening peoples is gone and the late supper peoples isn't come yet. Don' mention my name. Is delicate, you understand? Tell him you are a priest."

They left Gianni's on the whole well pleased with their work. They walked home, talking over the options, and when they arrived back at the vicarage they found that Stanko had spent the time vacuuming over the entire house. Their threadbare carpets hadn't looked so good for years.

"Just so long as he doesn't start clearing up my desk," said Paul, ruefully glancing at the chaos there.

They rang up Signor Gabrielli that evening, having been assured by Stanko — he regarded the question as almost insulting — that he made an excellent pizza. Paul took Gianni's advice and introduced himself as the "priest" of St Saviour's. Signor Gabrielli, amiable to start with, became positively friendly.

"Ah, you want pizzas? You want pizzas for a party?"

"Not at the moment, though it's an idea. Definitely an idea. No, it's a question of someone I'm trying to help."

"Yes?" Still friendly.

"He's not an Italian, but a Yugoslav. Bosnian, I suppose we should say. He's an excellent cook, makes a splendid pizza, and it's a question of whether you might have a job at Pizza Pronto."

There was a pause, and then a somewhat cautious response.

"I could do with some help, certainly some evenings."

"There are reasons in his case to be . . . discreet about the fact that you are employing him, if you understand."

"Ah yes," said Signor Gabrielli, his voice now low and conspiratorial. "Now I *do* understand."

"Particularly we need to be discreet because of where he comes from. The consequences of his being sent back there would be very much more serious than if he were sent back to Italy."

"*È vero.* In Italy we are not quite yet in the civil war. Maybe soon the North fight the South, but not yet. But the police they do send back to Yugoslavia, that I know."

"So we've heard. The important thing you understand, Signor Gabrielli, is not wonderful pay, but having enough to live on, and maybe a bed to sleep in. I don't suppose . . ."

"There is a room upstairs. Is not nice, is

partly storeroom, but it has a bed in it. Another boy — this is boy from Tunisia, you understand?"

"I understand."

"He has the other room. Is a nice boy, very clever with languages. So he is a companion. But perhaps I should talk to this man."

"Yes, of course. We wouldn't dream of suggesting you give him a job simply on my recommendation."

"Tomorrow evening, about this time, is possible he could come and we could talk?"

"Very possible. I shall be at a meeting, but my wife can bring him. Look, it might look best if we ordered a couple of pizzas. My wife can collect them, say at eight thirty, and Stanko can stay and talk when it's convenient for you."

"Excellent. What you like?"

"Let's say a Bologna sausage and a *quattro staggione.*"

"Right. I talk to your lady tomorrow."

Paul put down the receiver rather pleased with his work. He turned to face the others.

"It sounds very promising," he said to Stanko, who had followed with great relief the progress of the conversation. "There's a room above and another member of staff living there. In the same position as you, but it will *look* perfectly natural and normal. We don't want to be inhospitable, but —"

"You have been wonderful!"

"— but well, the fact is that everything a clergyman does is observed."

"And everything his wife does," said Rosemary. "By hawklike eyes."

The next night, when Paul was out at a meeting of Leeds clergy discussing the theme of "targeting young people," Rosemary and Stanko walked to the Ilkley Road and along to Pizza Pronto. As they neared the brightly painted little takeaway, Stanko, at Rosemary's suggestion, dropped back a few paces, and entered the warm, friendly place just behind her. As Rosemary went up to the middle-aged man behind the counter with a meaningful smile on her face, Stanko ducked under the counter and went to stand casually among the hot ovens and the table with bowls of chopped sausage and chopped mushroom and large tins of peeled tomatoes.

"Mrs Sheffield," said Rosemary. "The two I ordered."

Signor Gabrielli was friendly and respectful, but in a quite nonchalant way. Rosemary paid her money and went out bearing her comfortingly hot burden. She did not notice that among the little knot of people waiting for their orders was Selena Meadowes, and she certainly did not realise that Selena had been watching their approach all the way along the Ilkley Road.

# CHAPTER SEVEN

# *Whispering Campaign*

$S$tanko came back to the vicarage an hour later, but only to collect his clothes and belongings.

"I don't want to go," he said. "You have been so kind, both. But is better for you. The job is fine, the room is fine. I shall be quite all right."

"But you'll keep in touch," Rosemary insisted. "If you get any news from home you'll come round or ring? I'll give you our phone number."

"Is here," said Stanko, tapping his head.

He looked so slight and pathetic standing in the doorway that Rosemary wanted to give him a hug, as she might have hugged a son going off to school for the first time. But she resisted the impulse and told herself it was absurd: Stanko was experienced in the ways of the world — more experienced in its nastier byways than she was, in all probability. For a moment his gentleness and bewilderment seemed to her something like a triumph of the human spirit.

In the next few days Rosemary went about her business in the usual way, with that significant exception that she did not go to church. The omission, now several weeks long, left a hole in her life, but she found it difficult to pin down the nature of the void: was it a spiritual one or a social one? Or was it, perhaps, simply a matter of *time?* Sometimes she tried to fill the hole by walking to church to meet Paul as the service finished. That way at least she met some of the people she had been accustomed to meet. Mostly they were very kind and relaxed, but one evening she did note Timothy Armitage, an elderly and very devout parishioner, scurrying off in an unaccustomed direction, and she wondered whether he was trying to avoid her. Again, Mrs Mulholland, a middle-aged battle-axe, walked past her stony-faced one evening, but that was the sort of thing she did after the most trivial of slights: an omission to thank her for some small service, forgetting to enquire after her health when she'd been ill. Rosemary did not give it a second thought.

One evening, when Stanko had been gone nearly a week, after she'd been to tea with a housebound young mother, she turned aside from her shortest route home and went to see him in Pizza Pronto. Signor Gabrielli greeted her with a smile and took her hands in his.

"The boy makes a very nice pizza. He's very handy. You want to talk to him? I take over a bit."

And he went to where Stanko was juggling with little bits of this and that, scattering them blithely on to the dough base and laying shreds of ivory-coloured mozzarella on top. Stanko looked up, saw Rosemary, and came over, his face suffused with smiles. He had the gift of making people feel special.

"Rosemary! You are very kind."

"I wanted to see you. They said on the news there'd been an outbreak of fighting near Petrinje."

"Yes, I hear."

"You've had no news from your wife?"

"Nothing. I have a letter from my mother, but she hear nothing either."

"Is your mother in that area?"

"No. She is now in Zagreb. Is in safety."

"But she's no way of contacting your wife?"

"None." He looked up at her, with pain

in his troubled eyes. "Is horrible — not know-ing anything."

"It must be." She bent down, speaking ear-nestly. "*Please* ring us or come round if there is any news. The job here is all right, is it?"

"Is very nice. Always busy — that's what I need. I good friends with Hanif, and Mr Gabrielli is very kind. Don't you worry about me, Rosemary."

She smiled, said a hearty, encouraging good-bye, and left. She did not recognise any-body sitting waiting on the chairs around the counter: most of them were probably students or members of families where both parents worked — anyway, not members of the St Saviour's congregation. When she got home Paul was already back from one of his eternal meetings.

"I dropped in on Stanko on the way home from Maggie Pauling's," Rosemary said.

There was a tiny pause before Paul said, "Good. How is he getting along?"

Rosemary and Paul had been married for more than twenty-five years. Both of them knew in all its intricacy the grammar of mar-ital discourse. Rosemary understood perfectly the significance of that tiny pause, and Paul knew that he had let something slip and that she had understood what it was. Both of them decided it was something best not pursued until it was absorbed and all its implications comprehended.

It was a case, Rosemary decided, in which the best thing was to watch for signs and then interpret them. There had been talk, obviously, about her and Stanko. How did they know about Stanko, and how much did they know? She was more worried about that than anything they might imagine about the relationship between her and him. Dirty minds she could cope with, but there was the possibility that as soon as his nationality was known, someone would put two and two together and decide he was an illegal immigrant, or at least working illegally. Paul's was an intelligent rather than a warm-hearted parish.

The signs that she had decided to look for were not slow in showing themselves. They were ones that were usual in well-bred English circles: increased reserve or reticence in conversation, constraint in greeting, avoidance on social occasions. This was the British way not only of expressing disapproval of a supposed sin or crime, but also of sparing the disapprover the embarrassment of being open in their condemnation. It showed Rosemary that the person concerned had heard that she was having a fling, but it did not in any way pin them down as far as future conduct was concerned: if in the future the gossip proved groundless they could resume their relationship with her as if nothing had happened. In Italy ugly names might have been shouted at her in the street. In England people found urgent reasons for crossing to the other side of the road.

Rosemary observed and absorbed, as if she were studying British habits for a sociology course. She viewed this development surprisingly dispassionately as far as she personally was concerned. She was mainly worried about Stanko's plight. She rang Signor Gabrielli, who assured her that in the pizzeria Stanko was referred to as Silvio and that they conversed in the presence of the customers in an elementary kind of Italian.

"He speak a little, you know. We are neighbours, Italy and Yugoslavia, is a lot of tourism and he learns quickly. Is the same with my Tunisian. The buyers like to think these are Italian pizzas made by Italian boys — is natural."

Armed with this knowledge Rosemary felt she could talk the rumours over with somebody before she thrashed the matter out with Paul, in an attempt to decide whether to confront the gossip or just let it ride. She chose to visit Violet Gumbold, whose own marriage had been the subject of innuendo, based, so far as Rosemary knew, on little more than the fact that her husband was frequently away from home. Violet was getting around a bit more now but was still visited a lot by female parishioners, who stopped by for tea, biscuits and a spot of character assassination — in this respect parish behaviour had changed little over the last two hundred years. Rosemary found her in the middle of limb-strengthening exercises which she was very ready to discontinue. The pair of them sat in the kitchen, and Rosemary circled around the delicate subject.

"You'll soon be able to come back to church," she said.

"Next Sunday, I thought. People have offered me lifts, but I want to get there under my own steam when I do go. Pity you won't be there."

Rosemary grimaced.

"I have considered just going along — as a sort of habit, or in the hope that something will 'happen,' as I think Paul still hopes it will. It would fill a gap. But the idea of spending a lot of time on what has become an empty observance just doesn't appeal to me. There've got to be better ways of using my time."

Mrs Gumbold looked dubious.

"I suppose that's the practical view. But I do think it's sad. I hope you don't mind me saying that."

"Not in the least. But I have to say that for some reason — and it's odd, when you think how much of my life has been given to the Church, in one way or another — it's not sad for me. I feel *freed* from something."

"Well, I hope it doesn't last."

"I almost hope it does. Maybe it's the pleasure of being freed from some of the sort of people who do go to church."

She looked at Violet Gumbold out of the corner of her eye and saw that she took the point.

"Rosemary!" she said, beginning to blush. "You've always got on so well with us all in the past."

"Yes — well enough. But the relationship has never really been challenged on either side. Now it has been."

"By your loss of faith?"

"That, and this notion that I'm having an affair." Mrs Gumbold looked down into her cup. "And now that it is challenged, I'm afraid I'm weighing a lot of people in the balance and finding them wanting."

Violet Gumbold made no reply, though she was clearly trying to think of one.

"Is the whole parish talking about it, Violet?"

"Well, yes. I'm afraid they are." She seemed quite ready to talk as long as they stuck to facts.

"Without coming to talk to me about it?"

"I suppose they think you'd just deny it, there wouldn't be any point."

"Ah — the 'he would, wouldn't he?' syndrome. They must feel they have some pretty good evidence."

"I don't know about that. You have been seen to go to Pizza Pronto just to talk to him."

"Gosh! How sinful!"

"And it's said you introduced him to Mr Gabrielli and persuaded him to give the young man a job."

"Again, gosh. Come off it, Vi. They must be throwing around nastier stuff than that." Violet Gumbold was silent. Rosemary sighed. "All right, let's get on to the who. Who started all this talk?"

"Really, I couldn't say, Rosemary."

"You mean you won't tell me."

"No, I won't. But I will tell you what they're saying about how it started." She was still looking down at her cup, but she felt she had to look Rosemary in the face when saying it, so she raised her eyes. "They say it began when you went to Scarborough, and that he got the sack when he was seen coming out of your room one night."

Rosemary laughed.

"Right. Thank you, Violet. That's really what I wanted to know. You know, if it wasn't for poor old Paul and his position in the parish I think I'd find it rather flattering that someone my age could snap her fingers and have someone St — Silvio's age come running. But it doesn't seem much like real life."

"I don't know, Rosemary: affairs between older women and younger men seem very common these days."

"Only in the soaps. And they're *not* real life."

"It's not just the soaps. You read about it all the time. Show biz people and that. You're still a very attractive woman."

"The 'still' says it all."

"And he's a charming young man."

"You know him?"

"Well, I saw him when I was driven by Mrs Harridance to get a pizza."

Rosemary allowed herself a malicious smile.

"Funny, I've never thought of you as a pizza sort of person, Violet. Or Florrie, come to that. One good result of all this is probably that Signor Gabrielli's business has picked up no end."

"Oh Rosemary, you're being unkind. I don't *want* to believe these rumours, truly."

"Then don't. The trouble with rumours is that people get the idea that if they hear them often enough they must be true. This one is being circulated vigorously, you'll hear it often, but it is nonetheless a lie."

Leaving Violet Gumbold's Rosemary felt delighted that she'd pumped her: the information she had got was just what she wanted. It gave her, too, several possible avenues for further activity, at least one of them very enticing. It was by no means clear to Rosemary, though, how best to investigate the Scarborough connection, and it was not till the following afternoon, when she was alone in the vicarage, that she felt confident enough to ring up the Cliff View Guesthouse.

"Hello, that is Mrs Blundell, isn't it? This is Rosemary Sheffield — I stayed with you a couple of weeks ago."

"Oh yes, Mrs Sheffield." Cautious — not a good start. It threw Rosemary off course, and she blundered on less circuitously than she had intended.

"Mrs Blundell, I wanted to ask something about Stanko —"

"Oh, I couldn't possibly discuss any of my staff with you, Mrs Sheffield."

"I don't want to discuss him, Mrs Blundell. He's here in Leeds at the moment, and I can talk to him any time I want."

There was a slight access of warmth, as she added: "I hope he's found a job."

"Yes — he's working in a pizzeria."

"Good. I always liked him greatly."

"He says he was sacked because the police were clamping down on people working illegally."

"I couldn't possibly comment on that."

"Mrs Blundell, let's stop being cloak and dagger about this, shall we? I very much doubt if my telephone or your telephone is being tapped. I know and you know that Stanko has no work permit. Was this why you got rid of him?"

There was a brief silence, then some sign of cautious co-operation.

"When summer comes the police tend to get more interested, with all the hotels and guesthouses taking extra people on. I always make sure that all my staff have their papers in order during the peak months."

"Meaning July and August. So that wasn't why you got rid of Stanko now, in May?" There was silence at the other end, and Rosemary plunged on. "Mrs Blundell, there is a nasty rumour being spread around the parish, very distressing to my husband and me, that Stanko was sacked after being seen coming out of my room. The implications are obvious. Is that true?"

This time, after a pause, Mrs Blundell replied.

"No, that's not true. I can assure you of that, Mrs Sheffield. As you know, there was quite a while between your visit and my suggesting to Stanko that he move on."

"Exactly. But am I right in thinking that there was some kind of an incident?"

"Well . . . the fact is, Mrs Sheffield, that he *was* seen coming out of your room one evening — not late, as you will know, but — well, old people talk, and often they have rather nasty minds. When it came to me, this talk, I took no notice, because I knew you took an interest in him and his problems. But a lot of my guests are long-term in the winter months, and when the same people came to me with another incident of the same kind —"

"You mean Stanko coming out of a female guest's room?"

"Yes. Such a nice woman, really sweet, here for a few days with her mother. So anyway I felt I didn't have a leg to stand on, when it happened a second time, particularly as I'd told him to be careful, so I asked him to move on."

"You didn't talk to Mrs Meadowes about it?"

"No, I didn—" There was a shocked silence. "I did *not* mention any name, Mrs Sheffield."

"No, Mrs Blundell, you didn't need to. I am *so* grateful to you for clearing the matter up."

"So far as I know, Mrs Meadowes knows nothing about it — she and her mother left the next morning. I wouldn't want —"

"I shall be very careful, Mrs Blundell, very tactful. I can assure you of that. It goes with being a vicar's wife."

So that was that. Thinking about it as she put the phone down she wondered whether her closing remark hadn't been misleading: she was tempted to be very tactless indeed. In fact she was tempted to spread the rumour, or rather the news, that Stanko had been sacked after he had been seen leaving Mrs Meadowes's bedroom. That would certainly signify an end to turning the other cheek, but it would be both satisfying and poetically just.

A moment's thought convinced her that such a move could spell disaster for Stanko. The more attention that was focussed on him, the more likely it would be that he would be forced to make another quick move. The only safe course for Stanko was to fade into the background, and the really unfortunate aspect of Selena Meadowes's gossip was that it prevented him doing that. But how much did she know about him? Did she know anything about his place of origin?

Rosemary decided to find out. She also determined to have a showdown with Selena.

She had just made this decision, and was turning her mind to the when and where, when Paul came in from evensong. He seemed in fine good humour.

"I made a suggestion about the party after the spring fête," he said, rubbing his hands.

"Some genteel version of the rite of spring?" Rosemary enquired. "With me as sacrificial victim?"

"Ah yes — well, it did have something to do with that. All this silly talk — I know we haven't discussed it —"

"But we both know it's been going on."

"Exactly. Well, I thought that for refreshments, as a change, instead of going to the Cosy Nook people to do quiche and salad as usual, we'd get a big order of pizzas from Pizza Pronto. Everybody likes them, and it will make a change."

*"And?"*

"And I've organised with Signor Gabrielli that Stanko will bring them along to the parish hall. I'll be conspicuously friendly, I'll introduce him to people — as Silvio, of course — and *that* should stop people's tongues."

Rosemary saw no option but to kiss her husband and seem to applaud his notion. It seemed the only possible reaction to his puppyish, pleased-with-himself air.

"Dear old unsuspicious Paul! When I *do* decide to have an affair your simple trust will be an invaluable asset."

"You think it's a good idea?"

"Excellent. But don't imagine it will stop people's tongues. Nothing ever does that. But it may slow them down a bit."

But privately she thought that they would be drawing attention to Stanko, just when they ought to be letting him fade from people's minds. Because she was determined that Selena Meadowes was going to withdraw her slanders, and well before the spring parish party.

# CHAPTER EIGHT

# Party Going

*R*osemary bearded Selena Meadowes next day in her bland semi off the Otley Road, distinguished only by looped satin curtains in the front room, which made the bay windows look like a toy stage at which Selena might be expected to appear as Maria von Trapp and sing of her favourite things.

Rosemary marched up to the front door and gave a single businesslike ring on the doorbell. When Selena opened it with a nervous smile Rosemary said, "Hello Selena. I want to have a talk about what you've been saying about me."

Selena seemed inclined at first to bar her entrance, but Rosemary marched straight past her, down the hall and into the sitting room. Selena was alone in the house, luckily: her anonymous-looking husband was at work at his bank and her 2.5 children at school. She could be taken on in single combat.

Rosemary sat down in a fat armchair and had to resist the impulse to gesture to Selena to do likewise. Truth to tell, she was going to use to the full her seniority and her moral superiority. She felt rather like a headmistress preparing to give an almighty dressing-down to an unsatisfactory pupil.

"Right, Selena," she began, "let's not beat about the bush. You and I both know the rumours about me that have been put around the parish."

"Well, Rosemary, I have heard," said Selena, in her littlest voice, "but of course I would be the *last* person to spread anything like that."

"Don't pretend to be above gossip, Selena. Very few of us are that. And if not you, who else? You got the idea that I had been up to something in Scarborough — whether this was because you felt that someone who had lost her faith was bound to feel free of all restraint and go wild, or because you saw me happy and relaxed and put your own interpretation on it I can't guess. The last thing I'd care to do is go into your thought processes. But you went to Scarborough intending to find out any dirt that was going, and you succeeded. You heard — or by dint of questioning you learnt — that there had been comment on the fact that Silvio had been seen coming out of my room during the evening."

"Well, I must say Rosemary I was *most* surprised —"

"You were delighted, Selena: be honest with yourself for once. It was exactly the sort of information you'd hoped for. And then, when Silvio turned up in Leeds some days later, and when he and I were seen together, you put two and two together and made the sort of fantastic number people do come up with when they try to work out that particular sum."

Selena Meadowes dabbed at her eyes, which were dry.

"You're most unfair, Rosemary."

"I am, on the contrary, unduly charitable, since I haven't gone into your motives. Now, I have no intention of defending myself or explaining myself to you, Selena. I would only ever do that to someone I respected. What I insist on is that you use the same energy and devotion you've been using in spreading this story to retracting it. I want you to tell everyone that you've made a terrible mistake, that it was a result of a complete misunderstanding of what happened at Cliff View, and that you've been assured by the landlady that there's no question of Silvio having been sacked after being seen coming out of my room."

"But Rosemary," said Selena, a cunning look coming into her eyes, "that wouldn't be true, would it? I know the man — Silvio, is that his name? — *was* seen coming out of your room. And I haven't spoken to Mrs Blundell about it. You wouldn't want me to tell lies, would you?"

"Selena, after stretching the truth in the way you have in the last week or two, you can hardly jib at stretching it an inch or two further. You knew perfectly well, and ignored the fact, that there were weeks between my visit and Silvio being sacked. If you want to you can ring Mrs Blundell at Cliff View and find out the truth."

"Oh, that would be rather awkward."

"It would be *very* awkward for you. Because by chance you did hit on the truth about Silvio. He was asked to leave after being seen coming out of a guest's bedroom. Unfortunately the bedroom in question was yours, Selena."

For the first time she showed real emotion.

"Rosemary! It wasn't!"

"Oh but it was. No doubt you'd been asking probing questions about him and me. I haven't discussed that with him, not wanting to embarrass him. But it's unfortunate for you, isn't it? Because if you do not start retracting your story — vigorously, comprehensively, totally — I shall tell people the truth about Silvio's dismissal with a great deal of pleasure."

"You wouldn't!"

"You think not? I don't know how stable your marriage is, Selena. That wasn't something you thought about when you started spreading stories about me, and I won't greatly concern myself with it if I have to start spreading stories about you. But I wonder how Derek would feel if all the parish was talking about his wife and an Italian waiter. A bit conventional, your Derek, isn't he? And a bit of a snob as well, I would guess. Think about it, Selena, and if you're wise you'll start spreading your retraction, and making it as convincing as you know how. Time to do a bit of grovelling, I think, Selena."

So much for turning the other cheek, Rosemary thought, as she left the Meadoweses' bijou residence. Perhaps turning the other cheek needs to alternate at times with the threat of strong-arm tactics to be fully effective. In any event she decided not to give Paul anything but a very generalised account of her conversation with Selena.

There was one other reason for being satisfied with the interview, and this she could share with Paul. It was obvious that Selena had never bothered to find out Stanko's name when she was at Scarborough, or even his nationality. One less thing to be explained, one more dangerous possibility avoided. The main thing was that talk should die down, and Stanko be allowed to fade into the background.

Die down it did, somewhat to her surprise. Perhaps it had something to do with the fact that she had always been liked and respected in the parish, both for herself and as the vicar's wife. The retraction, as it progressed (much more slowly, inevitably, than the gossip), was believed: people stopped avoiding her, snubbing her, pretending she wasn't there. Though the retraction lacked the specificity of the original gossip — inevitably, since Stanko and his situation had to be kept out of it — it was accepted by most of those who had heard it. Perhaps it was the deadly earnestness of Selena Meadowes that did the trick.

Rosemary took the renewed warmth as she had taken the quiet ostracism, but just once she did say something. She had walked in the pale sunshine to meet Paul from St Saviour's and perhaps go with him to the Five Hundred Tavern when Timothy Armitage, emerging with the congregation, saw her waiting and made a point of coming over and greeting her.

"So good to see you, Rosemary. It's nice that you're not shunning us."

Remembering his scurrying off to avoid having to talk to her she said, "I won't shun you if you don't shun me, Timothy."

He looked down at the pavement.

"Oh, my dear, you noticed!"

"Of course I did. Gossip's so easy to believe, isn't it, even when you don't want to?"

"You make me feel very small, Rosemary. I feel that I've let you down."

"No hard feelings." To soften her words — because Timothy was really one of the nicest members of the congregation, and she had spoken as she had only because he was one of the ones who would understand — Rosemary added: "Remember me when Lassie has her litter. I think I'm ready for another dog."

"You *have* been out of things, Rosemary. She had them last week. Come round and see them when they're a bit bigger."

The shift in parish opinion gave Rosemary the hope that Stanko's appearance at the party after the spring fête would be unsensational. It couldn't be too much of a nonevent from her or from his point of view: talk about

Stanko almost inevitably meant questions about Stanko. Or Silvio, as she tried to call him, even in her own mind.

Meanwhile her children were coming up for the weekend of the fête and party.

It hadn't been planned like that. Or had it? Janet had certainly promised to bring her new boyfriend up during his half-term. Mark had said nothing about coming, but now suddenly he was too. Had there been collusion between the two? Recently there seemed to have grown up a closeness between them, which somehow Rosemary didn't like. Stop being paranoid, she told herself. Still, there was the possibility that Mark's antennae had caught the new gossip and he was coming up to smell out the lie of the land and give her a thoughtful little lecture in the phraseology of a *Times* leader. A *Times* leader of the Rees-Mogg era. If so, he could expect an explosion. There is just so much lecturing that parents can take from their children, Rosemary said to herself.

They arrived on the Friday before the fête and party. Janet and Kevin arrived in Kevin's old banger. Kevin was a cheery, fresh-faced young man, very different from Janet's former boyfriends, who had tended to be saturnine, smouldery types who seemed to be auditioning for roles in prewar films set in

Ruritania. Whether there was anything *to* Kevin, Rosemary couldn't decide. There certainly hadn't been anything to his predecessors.

Kevin was sleeping at friends'. Rosemary was sure this was to spare her and Paul embarrassment. She rather resented this sort of cossetting. She felt she could have coped with the idea that her daughter and her daughter's boyfriend were sleeping together.

Mark arrived by coach from Oxford with a prim little suitcase and a large bag of dirty washing. He was much as usual, only more so. He brought up Rosemary's loss of faith almost at once and at every subsequent opportunity thereafter. He was very dissatisfied with Rosemary's explanation that "it just went," but he failed to get much more out of her. He clearly had ambitions to be a Torquemada without any of the necessary skills.

Paul and Rosemary had agreed that something had to be said about the recent rumour-mongering. The opportunity came up on Friday night at dinner, when Mark asked how things were going on in the parish.

"Buzzing," said Rosemary, helping herself to more potatoes. "Someone has been spreading the rumour that I'm having an affair with a fast-food chef."

"Mother! You're joking!" said Mark.

"How exciting," said Janet. "I presume you're not."

"I don't think I'm flattered that you should presume that, but no, I'm not."

"How did the idea get around, though?" asked Mark, increasingly headmasterly.

"Let me see," said Rosemary, pretending to think. "I got him his present job. He was a waiter at my guesthouse in Scarborough. He was seen coming out of my room there at around half past nine one evening."

Mark puffed out his cheeks, already plump, and looked very concerned. Or looked, to be precise, like a turkey about to lay an egg.

"Mother, you haven't been silly, have you?"

"As a matter of fact I think I've been very responsible."

"You do realise, don't you, that with your loss of your Christian belief, people in the parish will be on the lookout for falling standards in other matters as well? You will need to be very careful not to do anything that could give rise to scandal. You should think about that."

"What does give me pause for thought, Mark, is the question of how it has come about that your father and I have somehow produced a pompous and sanctimonious little prat like you."

There was a silence, Mark went tomato-red, and Paul stepped into the breach.

"Would anybody like some more carrots?"

Later that evening, when she was helping Rosemary with the washing up, Janet said, "That was glorious, Mother. Absolutely spot-on."

But reaction had set in, and self-doubt.

"It was rather cruel, I'm afraid, and pre-meditated as well. I knew I was going to get a sermon from him."

"Yes, that was easy enough to guess."

"Anyway, why the congratulations? I thought you and he were rather close at the moment."

"Close? Good heavens, no."

"You just seem to be seeing more of each other."

"Well actually . . ." Janet shuffled a little, then gave her mother a little grin. "Kevin, you see, writes these little plays, one-acters, for his kids to perform at the end of term. The first time he met Mark he started badgering me to invite him to this and that — hence *Carousel*. He's put this wonderful prat, to use your word, Mum, into his present play, and Mark keeps pro-viding him with wonderful things to say."

"Well, it's nice to know he has his uses. Good for Kevin," said Rosemary, thinking that there must be more to him than to all those gigolo types who had preceded him. "Golly, I do hope this is just a dreadful passing phase with Mark. What I really worry about is the Church."

"The Church?"

"Well, I *do* care about it, in spite of what's happened to me. It's been my life up to now. Mark will be the most terrible clergyman if he goes on the way he is going — the congregation will defect in droves. There's no chance of his leaving over the ordination of women, is there?"

"None at all. He thinks it provides the most wonderful opportunity for renewal and revival."

"Oh dear. The Catholic Church does seem to be able to embrace awful people much more easily than the Anglican one. Look at all those dreadful politicians. Paul was talking about them only the other day. We seemed to give them a platform, whereas now they're Catholics they keep wonderfully quiet. . . . Tell Kevin he'll have to come to the church party tomorrow night. We can introduce him to lots more terrible types for his plays."

That night they all watched the ten o'clock news together. The peace processes in the former Yugoslavia were gathering momentum, and the guarded optimism of recent months was giving way to a sturdier hope. Rosemary was conscious that she was making an almost physical effort not to show more than a normal humanitarian interest. The truth of the lines about what a tangled web we weave was neatly illustrated in her case, though she told herself that her deceptions were quite selfless, designed only to benefit Stanko. Still, it didn't feel good to hold back such an important part of her recent life from her own children.

Fête days had an ordained pattern, an almost mechanical routine, like coronations or (for all Rosemary knew) bar mitzvahs. Who did what was known, and was varied only by illness, retirement or death. The fact that some members of the congregation were beginning to feel that they had done their bit would lead to changes in the Mothers' Union next year, but did not yet mean changes in the arrangements for the fête. The various ladies had their usual stalls, and the men understood their various backup functions without even being asked.

Rosemary, of course, had her allotted part in all this activity: fetching, carrying, filling in during tea breaks and pee breaks, getting change, transporting takings to the all-day safe at the bank, encouraging, exhorting and generally exhausting herself. The St Saviour's fête was genuinely popular, and people came in droves. It had a reputation for cheapness and quality, and Rosemary always saw people she did not recognise as residents of the area, let alone members of the congregation. Students came in large numbers too, in quest of cheap food. The hungry student was one of the phenomena of the nineties that Rosemary was saddest about: one of those revivals of an old tradition, like the worn-out working-class woman, which the country could do without.

She did manage — again, this was by tradition — a brief rest back at home around about five o'clock. Then it was up, change into her vicar's-wife uniform (olive-green woollen dress, calf-length, with a chunky necklace) then off across the park to the parish hall, where the party was always held, and where the preparations were already under way.

"Florrie! How nice to see you!"

Social occasions, in Rosemary's experience, generally began with a lie.

"Rosemary, you are looking well. But we've all said so all along, ever since you —"

"Are you doing the soft drinks as usual?"

"That's right: soft drinks free with the price of the ticket; glass of wine seventy-five pee."

135

She paused, thrusting out her bosom. "Mr Mills has got some very good value Bulgarian and Rumanian wines, I believe. Are you going to supervise the food as usual?"

"Yes I am."

"Pizza, I hear. So good that awkward little business is sorted out. I never believed it. Some people have terrible minds, don't they? Makes you ashamed to be human —"

Rosemary moved on mid-flow. The woman disgusted her, and she had the excuse of going about her business, which there was plenty of. Turning away she realised the encounter had been watched and overheard by Dark Satanic Mills.

"Good for you, Rosemary. I'm glad you stood up to them."

"*Did* I stand up to them?"

"I heard rumours of a visit to Selena Meadowes."

He nodded towards the centre of the hall, where the Meadowes family — Selena, Derek, and little Matthew and Flora — were clustered with some of the other younger people, having all the smiling anonymity of a family in a TV commercial.

"You know everything, Stephen. Is Dorothy here?"

"I expect she will be later, if the cat turns up. It went missing this afternoon, and she insists she's staying at home until it reappears."

"I know the feeling."

"She worries more about that cat than she does about me. It's not having children. . . ."

He said it resentfully, blamingly. Coming to the defence of a woman she hardly knew, Rosemary said, "If she'd had children she would worry about them more than about you. And quite right too, though you're probably the sort of husband who would resent it. Excuse me — I must go and get the plates and cutlery ready."

The long table had plates with serviettes at one end and knives and forks at the other. Rosemary had always resisted disposable plates and cutlery — the latter would have been even more than usually useless with pizza, and Rosemary expected that most people would use their fingers. She had three or four helpers already waiting behind the table, Violet Gumbold among them, and she chatted with them while observing how things were going in the hall. The party was filling up, with quite a lot of people paying at the door: as with the fête, the party had a reputation for offering good value. The congregation was actually outnumbered by nonworshippers, which suited Stephen Mills, who was standing by the table talking to local businessmen. Rosemary heard words like "cash flow," "liquidity" and "reserves." It occurred to her that she had only the vaguest idea what Stephen *did,* but she certainly associated him with expressions like "cash flow." She noticed how much more at ease he was with men of his own kind: with women, and with men like Paul, he tended to be actorish, conscious of being on display, with something of the difficult temperament of the peacock. With businessmen he shed all this and got down to brass tacks in a completely normal way. She decided he was a very old-fashioned kind of man.

Her nose twitched. Through the main door, where people were still strolling in and paying, Stanko had arrived, almost obscured by a great pile of large cartons from his hands to his chin. How good pizzas always smelt! Someone directed him to Rosemary's table, and he staggered over, smiling at her with his eyes. It was with relief that he lowered them on to the table.

"Thank you, Silvio," said Rosemary. "Can you help for a bit with cutting and handing out?"

She summoned her helpers round, and they began opening boxes. She noticed Paul approaching for his display of friendliness to Stanko for the parishioners' benefit. Stanko had grinned at her, nodded, and started round to her side of the table. He was passing Stephen Mills and his group when he realised he was being watched, and stopped. Rosemary looked up from her work of slicing pizza and saw too. Mills had broken off from his conversation and had his eyes fixed on the new arrival.

"Hello, Stanko," he said.

## CHAPTER NINE

# *An End and a Beginning*

*T*here were many accounts given subsequently of what happened next. There was no great disagreement about the facts, which were unexciting. What happened was that there was a moment or two's silence, in which Stanko seemed to be struggling to find something to say. Then he turned to Rosemary.

"I cannot stay to help. I sorry. Is many customers back at Pizza Pronto."

And he turned and hurried out.

Rosemary told the police (conscious that she was on the very outer verges of the truth, but without any guilty feelings about it) that Stanko had delivered the pizzas and left because they were busy back at the takeaway. Others recounted the encounter between him and Stephen Mills; but there were various versions of what Mills actually said, and the descriptions of Stanko's demeanour varied enormously: dumbfounded, guilty, outraged, angry, embarrassed were among the words used, and many suggested that Stanko was surprised to meet someone from his past whom he had betrayed or double-crossed, or by whom he himself had been betrayed or double-crossed. The encounter was so brief, it involved so few words, that there were as many accounts of it as there were witnesses. Rosemary, if she could have heard them, would have been surprised at the parish's holding so much imaginative energy.

She found it impossible to put the encounter out of her mind as she went through the mechanical business of slicing and distributing pizzas, but this did not prevent her from absorbing other things as well: how the party was going, how people were behaving. She noticed that her rebuke to her son had not significantly altered his manner: it was avuncular — avuncular at twenty-two! — and orotund. A certain tolerance was extended to him as the vicar's son, but she noticed that the people he talked at quickly found that there was something else it was imperative they do, or someone they simply had to talk to. Whereas her husband always had a crowd around him, her son mostly had a space.

When there was a lull in the work, when everyone was eating and before the washing up started, Rosemary was surprised to find herself bearded by Derek Meadowes. She had smiled at him, greeted him, often enough before, but this was the first time she could recall having anything approaching a conversation with him. He always reminded her of a minor public schoolboy, quite useful with a bat lower down in the batting order, with a mind the consistency of well-boiled cabbage.

"It's all going very well," he said.

"Yes, isn't it?"

"Everyone's worked very hard," he continued, dipping into his ragbag of clichés.

"It's a good parish for workers," Rosemary agreed.

"You seem to have been reinvigorated since your break in Scarborough."

"It was good to get away," said Rosemary, dipping into her own conversational ragbag but wondering all the time where all this was leading.

"Yes, Selena found that. It was nice of you to call on her the other day. You must have found a lot to chat about."

"Yes, we did." Rosemary, having found out where the conversation was leading, had no intention of obliging him with further information. For something to say she asked:

"Did your mother-in-law feel the benefit of Scarborough too? I believe she's failing."

"Mum? Failing? Good Lord, no. Plays golf three times a week and as strong-minded as they come. She's only sixty-one, you know. Prime of life."

"I must be thinking of someone else," said Rosemary meekly, but smiling to herself. "It's easy to get people mixed up in a large parish like this one."

"Good heavens, yes. I'd be doing it all the time if I was in your position. Er . . ."

Derek looked as if he was going to probe further, but then shut his mouth, obviously unable to find a suitably anodyne question that might lead Rosemary to tell him what had passed between his wife and her when she had called.

Pizzas had been eaten, quite a lot of wine drunk, and the washing-up beckoned. It was something she felt she did quite enough of at home. St Saviour's was a very forward-looking parish, but somehow this had never resulted in any males being part of the washing-up team. Rosemary took a deep breath, summoned her helpers and they went through to the kitchen and got stuck into it. Even working full out, with the efficiency born of long practice, it took them more than half an hour.

By the time they had finished, the party was thinning out a little but still had plenty of life left in it. There was a healthy queue at the wine table (did Britons drink more than when she was young, Rosemary wondered, or just drink more white wine?), and at the table where the pizzas had been served, there were a couple of students eating discarded fragments.

Her son Mark, Rosemary saw, had exhausted his store of other people's patience and was now talking to Janet and Kevin. His manner to them was much the same as his manner with other parishioners. She saw Kevin on occasion move back a step, to get a better look at his stance and his gestures. Sometimes she saw his eye flicker, as if he had heard something he wanted to remember.

It was cruel — both Kevin's using him for caricature and her own delight in it. And yet . . . Rosemary thought again about the cliché parents used, particularly when their children were going through "a certain stage": that they *loved* them but didn't *like* them very much. Was that possible? And if in fact she didn't love Mark, how had that come about?

Then she saw something that really put her on the alert. Janet was standing a little apart from her brother and her boyfriend, sipping at a glass of wine. Stephen Mills detached himself from a little knot of business-men, came over to her and bent his face close to hers. She fixed him with a stare of outrage and revulsion, then conspicuously turned away from him and went to stand closer to Mark and Kevin. Mills shrugged, smiling, and went off to find other people to talk money with.

The encounter troubled Rosemary. She had never before had reason to associate Janet with Stephen Mills in any sort of relationship at all. She had shared — she *thought* she had shared — the family's skepticism, that was all. But to account for that look, there *must* have been something else. It was worrying. She looked around her: her job was over. The party was going with a self-generating force towards its close. She decided to do what she often did when her parish duties were over: slip away home without any fuss. Paul was near the door, talking to Florrie Harridance. As she passed she winked at him and then passed out into the night.

She enjoyed the cool air and the quiet. She stuck to the road rather than crossing the dark park — these days an elementary pre-caution even for a far from nervous woman such as herself. As she walked on, her mind was going through the monotonous round of a single preoccupation: Janet and Stephen

Mills. Stephen Mills and Janet. Why did the idea disturb her so much, she wondered? Because she so disliked and distrusted Dark Satanic Mills, of course.

All was quiet at home. She poured herself a glass of milk from the fridge, then went straight up to bed. She felt totally exhausted and knew she would go straight to sleep and not wake up even when Paul joined her.

Nor did she. She slept right through until after eight. Paul, who presumably had been a lot later, was still fast asleep beside her. She slipped out of bed, put on a dressing gown, and started downstairs to get the morning tea. At the turn of the stairs she paused. Through the little window there she could see out to the park. At the wooded, hilly part to her left she could see police cars. There was a large area cordoned off, and a couple of uniformed men were keeping early-morning joggers and dog-walkers away. As she watched, another police car sped along the road beneath her on its way to the scene.

Rosemary shivered and went on down to the kitchen to make the tea.

# Part II

# *Charlie*

# CHAPTER TEN

# *Local Body*

*C*harlie Peace had been called on duty an hour before his shift was due to start. He lived with his girlfriend in a small flat about ten minutes from where the body was found. When he arrived there he found the area already cordoned off, with a small knot of uniformed men urging sightseers to move on, which they did with the unabashed reluctance of natural ghouls. The photographers and other scene of the crime men were hard at work in the immediate vicinity of the body. Charlie looked around for anyone from CID and saw on the other side of the fenced-off area his preferred boss, Mike Oddie, who was being approached by one of the S.O.C.O. men. Charlie went over to his side and surveyed the scene.

"You've cordoned off a big area," he said.

"Blood," said Oddie briefly, looking at the

things he had just been handed. "There was a trail of it."

"Long time dying? Long-running fight?"

"Maybe the latter. But it seems to have ended with his throat being cut."

"Unusual."

"Distinctly odd."

Charlie stood quietly, his eyes still fixed on the body and its surroundings. He was in a part of Leeds that in theory he ought to know well: it was close to home and he ran there three or four times a week — not obsessively, merely keeping fit for his job. But running does not encourage you to survey the scene. Mostly you keep your eyes on the ground, watching for muddy patches, glass or dog dirt. The body was on the rising ground at the far end of Herrick Park, where tended grassland shaded off into woodland. The body was on grass, but the cordoned-off area included the wide pathway between the trees. All this was no great way from the road, but if the killing took place at night the darkness made it unlikely that any passing motorist would have seen anything. Or indeed would have done anything if he had. Charlie looked over the expanse of green towards tennis courts and the rather fine old buildings of Herrick College beyond. He knew that few students went through the park area after dark — almost no female ones.

"Who is he?" he asked.

"According to his wallet someone called Stephen Mills. Ring any bells?"

"None."

"His business card is for European Opportunities Ltd. Private address and office address given. Know anything about the firm?"

"Never heard of them."

"Me neither. Look at this." He showed him a printed ticket for the St Saviour's spring party, for Saturday, May 15. Admit one. "Last night. Presumably that's where he'd been. Hardly the sort of rave-up you might expect to lead to this."

Charlie shook his head vigorously.

"Don't you believe it. Religious people are the biggest bearers of grudges around. Don't you know any churchgoers?"

Oddie thought.

"As a matter of fact, I don't. No regular ones, anyway. Sign of the times, I suppose."

"Well, they are. And they're very good at justifying themselves in their grudges." Having delivered himself of this wisdom with some relish, Charlie thought for a little. "Well now, we're getting to know our body: Stephen Mills, assaulted and killed on the way back from the St Saviour's spring party. I know about that party. My girlfriend told me that some of her friends were going."

"Oh? Religious? I didn't know Felicity was a churchgoer."

"She's not. The St Saviour's party is cheap, with lots of grub. There'd been a fête earlier on. It's known as a place where you can get good things at knockdown prices — jams, cakes and that sort of thing. Students are always on the lookout for cheap food. Any idea when this chap was killed?"

"Doc is cagey, as ever, but he says he's been there hours. I could have told him that. He's been rained on."

"The vicar of St Saviour's lives over there," said Charlie pointing to a part of the road a few hundred yards away. "I think his name is Sheffield. I could find the house easily enough. Want me to go and have a word?"

But as he spoke a figure in clericals came out of one of the houses, with a woman beside him. As they watched he kissed her, got into his car and waited for a moment. Two young people came out of the house in a hurry, got into the car, and it drove away, leaving the woman on the pavement.

"That's his wife," said Charlie, not afraid to state the obvious. "She sometimes comes out on to the park when she's seen him off to church." They watched as she crossed the road and walked towards the tennis courts, casting occasional glances in the direction of the police presence, as if she would like to join the curious public if it weren't for the fact that it was not the done thing. "Want me to go and have a word with her?"

"Do you know her?"

"Nodding acquaintances."

"Well, why not? Can't do any harm." Oddie thought for a moment. "I'll send someone now to this address to see if there's a wife and break it to her. Be a bit careful what you say to the vicar's lady, but see what you can find out about the church bash last night."

Charlie headed towards her, and when he saw her turn and start back towards her defiantly ordinary vicarage, he broke into a run. She heard him, looked around and, when she saw who it was, smiled.

"Hello. We sort of know each other, don't we?" she said.

"To nod and smile to."

"Were you wanting my husband?"

"Well, I may have to speak to him later."

"Births, marriages or deaths?"

"None of those at the moment, thank you. Actually it was you I wanted to speak to."

"Oh?"

"I'm from up there." He turned and pointed towards the impressive police presence on the knoll. Comprehension dawned in Rosemary's face.

"Oh, you're a policeman!"

"Detective Constable Peace."

She frowned.

"I don't know that I can help, I'm afraid. I slept well, didn't see or hear a thing."

"I thought you might have been at the St Saviour's party last night."

Rosemary raised her eyebrows.

"I was. I was helping with the food. What on earth can that have to do with anything?" She looked him in the eye. "What are you investigating up there?"

"I . . . can't be too specific —" Charlie began.

Light dawned on Rosemary.

"Of course. There are so many of you. It couldn't be anything but a body, could it?"

He returned her look guilelessly.

"If you could just tell me a bit about the party, Mrs . . . Sheffield, isn't it?"

"That's right. Of course you have to be careful, I can see that. Well, there's not a great deal to tell. It went off very well, as usual. I slipped away early."

"How early?"

"I don't remember exactly. A bit before ten, I think."

"Did you notice a Stephen Mills at the party?"

"Oh yes, I — oh dear. Is it him? But I suppose I'm not allowed to ask."

"You did notice him?"

"Yes, he was there. He was close by the table when I was going to serve the food. Then I saw him again later. Both times he was with a little group of men — business-men."

"They were close to you at the table, were they? Did you hear what they were talking about?"

"Oh, the usual things I imagine when busi-ness people get together: the dire state of the economy, whether there are any signs of things picking up. I caught some phrases suggesting that. It wasn't the sort of talk that interests me."

"It didn't develop into any sort of row?"

Charlie noted Rosemary looking up at him sharply.

"Good heavens, no."

"How did the group break up?"

"The food arrived, and everybody got plates and we began to serve it."

"And the later group?"

"I was too far away to hear anything."

"Was he still there when you left?"

Rosemary had a sudden sharp picture of

Mills going up to Janet, and the surprising rebuff he had received.

"Yes, I'm pretty sure he was still there," she said.

"Could you tell me the names of the businessmen he was talking to, if I should need them?"

"One or two. They weren't all churchgoers by any means, but I expect if I were to get together with the other women who were serving the food we could come up with most of the names."

"I got the impression . . ." Here Charlie paused, having difficulty in finding an appropriately roundabout way of putting his impression into words, "that when you made your assumption about Stephen Mills you — well, let's say either you weren't surprised, or you weren't upset."

In spite of the tentativeness of his words Rosemary suddenly sensed something formidable about Charlie and realised she had to go very carefully.

"Certainly I was surprised," she said. "Sudden death is always surprising, isn't it? . . . If that's what it is. . . . But yes, if that's what it is I suppose I shan't be too upset. It sounds unfeeling, but that's the truth."

Charlie smiled encouragingly. He had not

expected such honesty from a vicar's wife.

"You didn't like him?"

"Not much. And didn't trust him either."

"Why not?"

Rosemary paused before replying.

"Oh dear — this is going to sound silly. Because he was *too* handsome, *too* smooth, *too* ingratiating. He always had for me the air of a fraudster, a con man, a sharper."

"But you've no evidence that's what he was?"

"None at all."

"And he was a member of your husband's congregation."

"He was indeed. He'd been coming to St Saviour's for years. . . . Congregations include all sorts."

"Of course they do. What did he do for a living?"

"Business of some kind — I've very little idea what."

"Did he have a family?"

"He had a . . . Goodness, we have gone into the past tense, haven't we?" She registered Charlie's expression of annoyance with himself and went on hurriedly: "That's between ourselves. He has a wife. She comes to church now and then, but she isn't regular, not these days at any rate."

"But he is? Every Sunday?"

"Pretty much so. And quite active other-wise. Also in with other bodies such as the Rotarians, helps with the local youth groups, and so on."

"Sounds a model citizen."

"Oh, no doubt he . . . is. Don't take any notice of a cynical old body like me."

"But you think he's in it for what he can get out of it?"

"Yes, I'm afraid I do."

"What could that be?"

"Well, with groups like the Rotarians and the Masons it's pretty obvious, isn't it? No need for me to spell it out. With the Church I'm not at all sure. I've often asked myself, but I've never come up with an answer."

"You sound as if you've thought a lot about Mr Mills."

It was a sudden, sharp jab. Rosemary said, too hurriedly: "Oh, that's putting it too high. But he intrigued me. Intrigues me."

"I must be getting back," said Charlie. "My boss will probably want to talk to you and your husband later." But he paused in the act of turning away. "I saw you standing here one Sunday about a month or so ago. This sounds silly, but you looked . . . quite strange. As if you were having some kind of expe-rience. Or maybe a vision. Something mys-tical, it looked like."

"Yes, I remember. Goodness, how embarrassing. Was it so obvious? I remember thinking I was making an awful exhibition of myself. How awful! It makes me feel sort of spiritually naked."

"I was right? It was a mystical experience?"

"In reverse. Very much in reverse. I suddenly realised I no longer believed in God."

"Just like that? Belief just . . . left you?"

"Yes. That exactly describes it. When you saw me I was suddenly alone, without God. That was the beginning. . . ."

She stopped. He watched her closely.

"Of what?"

"Oh, of a lot of nastiness in the parish. You can imagine what people have been saying. I mustn't keep you. I'll tell my husband you may want to talk to him."

She walked on towards her semidetached vicarage, and Charlie wondered why he had been given what amounted to a dismissal. It was as if she had declined to enter what could be an area of danger. When he got back to Mike Oddie and the activity around the body, he said, "Interesting."

"What she told you, or the woman herself?"

"Both. But she's keeping something back."

"She knew him, did she? Maybe she disliked him. Murdered people tend to be disliked."

"She did know him, but she's not keeping back the fact that she disliked him. She made that perfectly clear."

"What did she tell you about him?"

Charlie ticked off each piece of information on his fingers.

"Local businessman, business unknown, keen churchgoer, reason unknown but probably not ardent faith. Smooth, good-looking, likes to keep in with people, particularly other businessmen. Has a wife but no family."

"And he was at the parish party?"

"Yes, and still there when she left, towards ten."

"Anything else?"

Charlie thought for a moment, feeling he was not yet at the heart of Rosemary's reticence.

"There seems to have been something going on in the parish recently. Some nastiness or other. It seems to have started with Mrs Sheffield — the vicar's wife, that is — losing her belief in God."

"Good heavens, that must be awkward. Like a surgeon's wife taking up alternative medicine."

"Yes. I get the impression the nastiness in the parish is not just about that, though. Some other factor has entered in. And she doesn't want to talk about it. She chatted quite happily about the loss of faith, but she cut the conversation short when we seemed to be straying towards other matters."

"Then we'll have to talk to some of the parishioners, won't we? In the meantime we'll have to talk to Mills's wife. As soon as we find out how she's taken the news I'll decide if it's worth going there when we finish here."

"I have the feeling that his wife was a bit of an irrelevance in Stephen Mills's life," said Charlie thoughtfully. "A sideshow, an optional extra."

"Why do you think that?"

"I got the impression he was the parish Lothario."

"Good Lord — I find it difficult to imagine any such thing."

"You just don't know anything about religion," said Charlie.

# CHAPTER ELEVEN

# *The Little Wife*

The Millses lived in a substantial, square Victorian house which gazed out at the world like one of the industrialists of the time: hard, confident, holding his secrets. Bentham Road was a "good" street off the Ilkley Road. The house had ample gardens around it and was shielded from curious gazes by trees and hedges. The imposing bay windows, curtained, on either side of the front door clearly belonged to large, formal rooms; further back the symmetry of the facade was lost, giving way to a more rambling, built-onto structure. It was a large house for two people and, built in a cul-de-sac, very quiet. It was even quieter than usual that day.

Mike Oddie had ascertained by telephoning the WPC on duty there that Mrs Mills would talk to them. He was told that she would prefer to get it over. When they rang the front doorbell the young woman who had fulfilled the traditional role of comforter opened it to them and beckoned them into the living room.

"She's upstairs — a bit upset, I think."

Oddie raised his eyebrows at the inappropriate cliché. He and Charlie looked around them. The room was not quite what they expected, being full of old furniture, including bookshelves with well-thumbed books and worn carpets and rugs. Charlie wondered whether it was a room that Stephen Mills had come into, rather than one he had made himself. It certainly wasn't a room that suggested the usual modern businessman, still less the parish Lothario.

"How did she take the news when you broke it to her?" Mike Oddie asked.

"Very well . . . more dazed than anything else," said Constable Morrison. "Kept asking questions about the details, but not crying or anything. When I told her you'd be coming soon she said she'd go upstairs and get tidy, but she went into the bathroom, and I've heard crying."

"That's a pretty common sequence."

"Oh, I don't need you to tell me that," said the woman, with a trace of bitterness in her voice. "I've had my share of breaking bad news and holding hands afterwards. It's a burden that ought to be shared more equally."

She looked at Charlie, who bared his teeth in one of his more fearsome smiles, designed to suggest in this case that as a comforter he was a nonstarter.

"Should I go and tell her you're here?" Morrison asked. But even as she spoke they heard the sound of soft footsteps coming down the stairs.

When she entered the room their first impression was of someone small and insignificant. She had put on a dark grey skirt and a cream blouse with halfhearted bits of frill here and there. Her eyes were red and she had no makeup on, though her hair, nondescript brown, had been neatly combed back into a little bun at the neck. It was only when Charlie looked into the reddened eyes that he saw how large, dark and beautiful they were. It was like diving into a pool and discovering it was bottomless.

"Hello. I'm Dorothy Mills."

Oddie shook her hand.

"I'm Superintendent Oddie, and this is DC Peace."

"Please sit down. I'd like to get this over so I can be alone and start to come to terms with it." She gestured them to seats, worn but comfortable like the rest of the furniture, and sat down herself. "Could you perhaps tell me a little about what happened? Constable Morrison has been very kind, but she couldn't tell me much. I do need to know where he was found and what . . . what had been done to him."

"Of course I'll tell you what I can," said Oddie. "He was found on the edge of Herrick Park by one of the early-morning joggers. He had had his throat cut. He'd been dead for some hours when he was found."

"I see." The words came out calmly, but she dabbed at her eyes as if the calmness was an effort. "Oh it all seems so . . . incredible, so *impossible!* I mean, Stephen was perfectly capable of looking after himself. How could he — this sounds silly — how could he *let* someone cut his throat? Was it someone who came up behind him? Was it someone he knew and trusted?"

"There had been a fight."

There was silence. She looked down into her lap.

"Oh dear. I wish it had been sudden. . . . I suppose he was on his way home from the St Saviour's party?"

"That's certainly what it looks like."

"I should have gone." Her hands began working as she started to blame herself — pudgy, unglamorous hands, hands that worked around the house. "Not that I could have done much, I suppose, if there had been a fight." She looked up at them again. "But we wouldn't have walked back through the park if I'd been with him, would we?"

"Why didn't you go?"

"The cat was missing, and I didn't want to go out before he turned up. . . . To tell you the truth, with these church do's Stephen usually bought two tickets to support them financially, but I was never frightfully keen."

"Aren't you a churchgoer?"

"An occasional one. I *used* to go, because Father was keen, but I suppose I got bored. It was the opposite of the usual in our household. Stephen was the churchgoer, and he'd take Dad when he was up to it."

"Your father lives with you?"

"Yes — he has a little flat at the back."

"So you and he were together last night?"

"Not together, but I was in and out to see how he was, and to give him a bit of supper and a cup of Ovaltine."

"You didn't go out looking for your cat?"

She looked at him with her unfathomable eyes and then over to Charlie Peace.

"No, I didn't, except just up and down the road here. If you go further you just find him by the front door when you get home after hours of looking and calling. . . . I do see where these questions are going, Superintendent. I wouldn't have gone to Herrick Park to look for him. He never goes that far away, and he'd have had to cross the Ilkley Road to get there. He's scared of busy roads, and he'd never have done that."

Oddie nodded, neutrally.

"He's home now?"

"Yes. I found him in the front garden about half past ten."

All this was delivered in a firm but dull voice, but one that occasionally broke, paused for a moment, then resumed again its apparently calm course.

"Mrs Mills, what did your husband do?"

She sat back in her chair as if expecting the question, acknowledging his right to ask it.

"He ran his own business, advising manufacturing firms about export opportunities in Europe and around the world. It was his own idea, and he built it up from nothing. He thought British businessmen fall behind because they are poor at foreign languages and they don't understand the needs and preferences and customs of other countries. They treat Budapest as if it's Whitehall and get nowhere as a consequence. He offered the sort of expert advice they needed. Stephen was very widely travelled, and he had friends and contacts everywhere."

"He was often away from home?"

"Not so much in recent years, but earlier, when the business was starting up. In the last few years, with everything in place, he's found he can do much of it by telephone or fax."

"Was it a business in which he would make enemies?"

"*No!*" At that the voice really broke. "No! Why should it make him enemies? He was just giving a service. He wasn't competing with anyone. . . . I keep trying to make sense of this in my mind. It would have been so much easier if he had been ill, if he had died naturally. Stephen didn't have enemies. He was so active, busy in all sorts of things, and he made friends, not enemies!"

He didn't make a friend of Rosemary Sheffield, Charlie thought to himself.

"How did you get to know him?" he asked.

"Through the church, mainly," she said, turning to him her deep eyes and unremarkable face. "As I say, I used to go much more regularly because I went with Dad. He's always been keen, particularly after Mother died. That was when I was ten, and I suppose he was looking for an interest to fill the gap.

168

So it was at St Saviour's that Stephen and I met."

"Where was he from? Did he have any family?"

"Not still alive. Both of his parents were dead."

"Where was he from?"

"London. South of the river."

"Was there any special reason why he moved to Leeds?"

"To get out of London, but still to have city amenities — theatre, music and so on." She smiled reminiscently. "I remember talking to him about that when we were engaged. Stephen had a very sharp eye. He could see then that Leeds was a much better proposition for the future than Manchester or Birmingham."

"And so he set up his business, and it did well," Charlie continued. "Was it still doing well? Businesses are going to the wall everywhere."

"It was — is — doing wonderfully well. There are all these new markets opening up in Eastern Europe. They want business know-how, and the British want to get into their markets. Oh no, the business is going better than ever."

"Who will take it over?"

She shook her head.

"Oh dear. I hadn't thought about that at all. . . . There's Brian Ferrett, his second in command. Perhaps he'd buy me out, or go on running it for me. . . . I can't say anything about that because I simply haven't had time to consider."

"I shouldn't have asked," Charlie said quietly. "Of course it's much too early for you to have thought of that."

"You see we're in a quandary," resumed Mike Oddie. "Someone has murdered your husband, and yet you can't think of anything that he's done that might have made him enemies."

"But I can't! It was a unique business where he had no competitors, and he and Brian Ferrett got on very well. . . . I just can't think of anyone who'd do *that*."

Oddie tried to put the next question tactfully.

"There are areas in his life you don't know so well. If he travelled a lot . . . and of course the church."

An expression came over her face that could only be described as mulish.

"I went to church now and then. I know the people there. Stephen did a lot of work for the church in all sorts of ways. If anyone resented him, then they'd be very ungrateful. But I don't believe for a moment they did."

"And the travelling?"

The mulish expression remained set.

"As I said, he'd done much less recently, now the business was up and running. Probably not more than three or four times a year, short trips, within Europe."

"Your husband was a handsome man," put in Charlie.

She had to suppress a flush of irritation.

"Please don't treat me as if I were stupid," she said sharply. "I can see the direction of these questions. You are a good-looking man, Constable. Does that mean I should take it for granted that you are stringing along five or six women at once?"

"No, but it means that if I wanted to I'd find it easier than someone who wasn't. I'm sorry if I offended you. I just meant that if he travelled a lot he might have had . . . relationships you knew nothing about."

"You're not making things any better, Constable."

"We weren't just thinking of . . . that kind of relationship," said Mike Oddie, stepping in quickly. "Eastern Europe is a pretty murky area at the moment. Take Russia, for example: gangsterism is rife there — big-scale, highly organised gangsterism. There are some seriously rich people, and most of them didn't get that way by straightforward capitalist enterprise."

Mrs Mills shrugged.

"That's the sort of thing I've just read about in newspapers. I'm quite sure Stephen would never get involved in it."

"The big men there need contacts in the West."

"They'd find they couldn't use Stephen — if they ever tried."

"Your husband may have found that, with his job, he couldn't keep out of involvement."

"You can always keep out of crime if you're firm about it. I think you're straying into fantasy, Superintendent."

"I'm just trying over possibilities in my mind, Mrs Mills."

"Talk it over with Brian. Look at the firm's records. I know you'll find everything was above board because that's the sort of man Stephen was. He was sharp, competitive and totally honest."

"I've heard mention of the Rotarians," said Charlie.

She turned to him, this time more openly hostile.

"Good heavens — are they considered suspicious now? Britain's Cosa Nostra?" She thought. "Stephen had been a member of the local branch for about seven years. A week or two ago he took over as treasurer from the Reverend Sheffield. That does not suggest that anyone in the Rotarians thought he was a dodgy character. But of course if you regard the whole organisation as suspect that won't cut any ice with you, will it?"

"I'm sorry. I seem to have the knack of offending you," said Charlie, with no obvious contrition.

"I'm sure you know your job," said Dorothy Mills. "But you don't know my husband."

"No, we don't know your husband yet," said Charlie quietly. He laid no particular emphasis on the last word, and she gave no sign of having registered it, but her next words seemed to be a response.

"He's hardly cold, and you seem to be scrabbling around trying to find out dirty secrets about him."

"It's what happens in a murder enquiry, I'm afraid," said Oddie.

"Haven't you thought that this may be casual, unmotivated violence?"

"That doesn't usually happen to healthy white males," said Oddie. "It happens to women, and the springboard, one way or another, is usually sexual. But of course we'll keep all possibilities in mind."

She swallowed.

"I suppose you want . . . Do you want me to . . . ?"

"Identify the body. Yes, I'm afraid we will want that, when you feel up to it."

"One gets such a knowledge of things, doesn't one, from the television and books, but you never think it's going to happen to you. . . ." She paused, then made a decision. "I would like to do it now, if that's convenient . . . get it over with, start again, or try to think about starting again. . . ."

"Yes, of course," said Oddie. "Could I just ring and find out if . . . everything is in order?"

"The telephone's over there." She gestured to a corner of the sitting room where it sat on a small table. As Oddie was dialling the number the door to the hall opened and an old man came in. He had been tall, commanding, but his big, lean frame was now bent. His face was Scandinavian — big-boned, with sunken cheeks; but the chin was still firm and determined, like the last stones of a once-proud house.

"What's happening, Dot?" he said, looking from Charlie to Oddie, then back at his daughter. "Why are these men here?"

She got up quickly and went over to him.

"Sit down, Dad. We've had some bad news. Would you like your cup of tea?"

174

"I've had my cup of tea. You know I can make my own tea, Dot." He sat down, under a sort of protest, but almost sighing with relief. "What do you mean, bad news?"

She knelt in front of him.

"It's dreadful news, Dad. Stephen had an accident coming home from the party last night. I'm afraid he's dead."

His mouth dropped open.

"Dead? Stephen dead? Dottie, he can't be."

"I'm afraid he is, Dad." She took his hand in hers and stroked it. "We've all got to be very brave. I've got to go and identify the body now."

"Oh Dot, how terrible for you. I can't believe it, though. Stephen dead. Dottie, tell me it isn't true."

He looked at her, bewilderedly, and seemed to see in her face that it was true. First one tear, then another, started coursing down his cavernous cheeks, and he began fumbling in his trouser pocket for a handkerchief.

"Poor Stephen. How can Stephen be dead? He was like a son to me. The only son I had. The best son I could have had."

It was, Charlie thought, the most grief he had yet seen displayed for Stephen Mills. Because he was not entirely convinced that what Dorothy Mills felt was grief.

Mike Oddie gestured to WPC Morrison to

stay with the old man, and together they led
Mrs Mills out to the car. Twice on the journey
into Leeds she made as if to ask something,
then stopped herself. It was as they were
drawing up at the West Yorkshire Police
Headquarters that she said, "Is he going to
look very dreadful?"

"They'll have cleaned him up as far as they
can," said Oddie. He adopted a businesslike
tone because experience told him that was
best. He led the way briskly inside. As they
passed the desk the duty sergeant hailed him.

"Call for you, Mike."

"Take it, Charlie, will you?" Oddie said,
and went on at the same fast pace towards
the police mortuary. Charlie picked up the
phone.

"DC Peace speaking."

"That's a constable, isn't it? I want to speak
to the man in charge."

"Superintendent Oddie is in the mortuary
with a witness who is identifying the body."

"Oh, that'll be Dorothy Mills, like as not,
I suppose. How is she taking it? Well, I suppose you won't be able to say much, especially
being junior, and I'll be brief with you, because I've got a Sunday dinner to cook. . . ."

Lancashire, thought Charlie, whose ear had
refined itself in his three years in the North.
And he very much doubted whether this lady

was going to be brief.

"Now, of course the whole parish is devastated by the news, particularly as he was among us last night, and when you've been speaking to a man — not that I said more than 'hello' — you can't believe, can you, that — ?"

"Excuse me, but we are *very* busy here. Could you get to the point?"

"That, young man, is *precisely* what I am getting to. My time is valuable if yours isn't. The point is the incident that happened at the party last night, when the food arrived. I thought you might not have heard about that."

"No, as a matter of fact we haven't, Mrs — ?"

"Harridance. Florrie Harridance."

"And address?"

"It's in the book. There's only one Harridance. Don't interrupt me, young man. *Now*, it was pizzas last night, and I can't think why, because it's never been pizzas before, and you can make what you like of that, because the person who brought them was this young man from Pizza Pronto that there's been all this talk about. Not that I give the talk any credence, because I *know* Rosemary Sheffield, and I know she never would, not with someone so young. Though people say it's her time of life, and we all know people do funny things —"

"Did the incident involve Mrs Sheffield?"

"It did *not*. Or not directly. Don't be foolish, young man. It involved Stephen Mills, or why would I be ringing you? The boy came in with cartons of that foreign rubbish piled high in his arms, and he dumped them on the table, and it was then that it happened."

"What happened?"

"He saw Stephen Mills, and Stephen Mills saw him."

"And?"

"They were doomfounded. Well, the boy was doomfounded. Stephen Mills was very cool — he was always very cool, was Stephen — what you'd call a cool customer. Any road, all he said was 'Hello, Stinker,' or that's what it sounded like, and the boy, this Silvio, he just stammered something and turned and ran out."

"I see. Is that all?"

"Well, by all accounts the expression on that young man's face was *murderous*."

"You say 'by all accounts.' Didn't you see it yourself?"

"No, I didn't. I wasn't close enough to see."

"And yet you were close enough to hear?"

"No, I was not, young man. What I've been telling you is what I've been told by those who were, and I've told you because it's not everyone who's public-spirited enough to come forward and volunteer information. If you want to talk to someone who was close by and who could both see and hear, you should go not to Mrs Sheffield, who may have her own reasons for not telling the whole story, but to Mrs Gumbold, that's Violet Gumbold, in Severn Road, and no I don't know the number but it's in the book and it's an unusual name like Harridance, so use your initiative. And now, young man, if you've nothing more to ask me of any consequence, I'm going to go and turn the potatoes over —"

"Feel free," said Charlie, and put the phone down quickly.

# CHAPTER TWELVE

# *Liars*

When Oddie came back from the mortuary he ushered Mrs Mills out to the waiting car, driven by a comfortable-looking sergeant, then came back into the headquarters' outer office.

"How did she take it?" Charlie asked.

"Very well. They'd done a good job on him. She just nodded. She's got herself well under control."

"Yes. . . . That phone call —"

"Oh yes. Anything interesting?"

"It was a woman who claimed there was some kind of incident while the food was being served at the party last night. Some kind of encounter between Stephen Mills and the young man who brought the food."

"Anything in it?"

Charlie frowned in puzzlement.

"I don't know. If I'd just heard the story

in isolation I'd have said she was making something out of nothing very much. But it's interesting that Mrs Sheffield didn't mention it."

"If it was nothing, why should she?"

"You're being literal-minded, Mike. There was some kind of a situation, an eyeball-to-eyeball thing. The boy was, according to this woman, disconcerted, and fled like a rabbit. Apparently there's been talk in the parish about him and Mrs Sheffield. What were you planning to do next?"

"Go to the offices of European Opportunities Ltd. I've got the address and Brian Ferrett's home phone number. I think I'll just commandeer all the papers I can lay my hands on, then bring Ferrett in here and see what I can get out of him. If I take a uniformed man with me I can give you a couple of hours, if you want to follow up this encounter."

"Done!" said Charlie happily. He turned to the nearest woman with a computer. "There's a Mrs Gumbold in Severn Road. Could you get me her number?"

When Charlie arrived at the Gumbolds' he found both of them at home. Sunday was one day, Mr Gumbold explained, when he could usually get back from his job as a rep for a paper firm. He was overweight, probably from too much driving and sitting. The pair had heard about the murder on the parish bush telegraph, and Mr Gumbold left Charlie with his wife, saying he'd only got back at midnight and wouldn't be of any use.

Violet Gumbold was fadedly pretty, honest if Charlie was any judge, but not too bright and probably easily led. When asked to say exactly what happened at the party when the pizzas arrived, she became hesitant.

"Of course I've talked it over with people, told my husband, but it's so difficult to remember exactly what I saw, putting aside what people have said. . . . The young man came in, with a great pile of cartons, brought them over to the table where we were. . . . I'm trying to *see*. . . ."

"That's good. Picture it all. Where was Stephen Mills?"

There was a pause. She really was trying.

"With two or three other men, to the young man's left. . . . The Reverend Sheffield was coming forward, I think intending to be friendly to the young man. . . . Then Rosemary — that's Mrs Sheffield — asked the young man if he would help cut up and serve the pizzas."

"Did he say yes?"

"I can't remember him saying anything, but he started forward, and then . . . then he saw Mr Mills, and he was — well — *thunderstruck,* I'd say. As if . . . well, as if he was the last person on earth he would have wanted to see."

"Did he look guilty?"

"That must have been it, mustn't it? Someone from his past whom he'd cheated or done down."

She seemed to have seized on that explanation. Charlie said, very gently, "You don't sound entirely convinced. Has someone suggested that to you? Wasn't that how it looked?"

She frowned.

"Well, somehow it wasn't. I can't really say that the boy looked guilty."

"Try to *see* it again. Try hard. How was it he looked?"

After a pause she said, "More outraged. Angry. And yet confused at the same time."

"Thank you. That's very helpful. So what happened next?"

"Mr Mills said 'Hello —' and then what I think was his name. It wasn't 'Stinker,' like people are saying, but something like that. Though people have been saying his name is Silvio. Anyway, the boy stammered something about them being busy back at the pizza place, and he turned and fled, though I'm sure he'd been intending to come and help us."

Charlie thought, fixing the picture in his mind.

"What was the expression on the boy's face as he left?"

"I couldn't see that. He turned and went away from us."

Charlie was inclined to put the murderous expression down to the embroidery endemic in parish gossip.

"You said the Reverend Sheffield was coming over intending to be friendly. Why should he take pains to be friendly with the deliveryman?"

Violet Gumbold looked confused.

"Well, of course he's naturally a nice person, and courteous . . ." Charlie fixed her with an unrelenting stare. "And you see there was all this silly talk. . . ."

"Tell me more."

She swallowed and went red.

"Well, actually it was about poor Rosemary and this young man from Pizza Pronto."

"The vicar's wife and the fast-food cook. It sounds like a dirty story. I presume it *was* a dirty story."

"Well, yes. People were saying —"

"I can guess what people were saying. Who was spreading the story?"

"Oh, I don't know about spreading —"

"Let's not quibble. Where did the story start?"

"I wouldn't want to accuse anyone. I'd much rather not say."

Charlie sighed.

"Mrs Gumbold, if this story was going round the parish I can find a hundred people who will have heard it, of whom I guarantee ninety will be willing to tell me who was spreading it. It's all one to me if you want the reputation of obstructing the police rather than helping them."

There was a long silence. Mrs Gumbold was a naturally law-abiding person. Finally she swallowed.

"Mrs Meadowes. It must have started with Selena Meadowes. I'm sure she meant no harm, but she'd been to Scarborough, you see, at the same guesthouse where Mrs Sheffield had gone when she lost . . . when she lost her faith, and this young man was a waiter there, and she heard talk about . . . about his having been seen coming from her room. That's what everyone was saying. And then he turned up here and Mrs Sheffield found him a job. . . ."

"So this Mrs Meadowes put two and two together and broadcast the result. Sounds like a really nice little congregation at St Saviour's."

"Oh, you mustn't think too badly of us. And I never heard it from her. She probably mentioned it to someone and it just . . . got around. And when she found out she was mistaken she went round to everyone to take the story back and say she'd wronged Rose-mary."

Ho, thought Charlie. And there again hum.

"And what was behind all this mudsling-ing?"

"Behind it?"

"Why were they so keen to do the dirty on Mrs Sheffield? She seems a very nice lady."

"I wish you wouldn't use . . . I couldn't say . . . It's not for me . . ." Fixed by Charlie's stare again, she hurried on: "Well, there are people who say they wanted her out of her parish positions so they could take over themselves."

"They?"

"Well, Mrs Harridance, Selena, and one or two others."

When he left Mrs Gumbold's Charlie felt very much more wised up on parish matters than when he had gone there. A seething mass of ambition, dirty tricks, slander and innuendo, or so it seemed. This didn't sur-prise him. It would not have been very dif-ferent in the predominantly black parish in his native Brixton with which he was well acquainted. His mother had fulfilled the double purpose of both spreading and providing the subject matter for a great deal of the gossip.

Charlie parked his car in a cul-de-sac off the Ilkley Road and walked along to Pizza Pronto. It was a takeaway he and his girlfriend had used in their time, though it was not the best in the area. He found it overflowing with waiting customers: word had obviously got around that there was a connection between it and the murder which was occupying everyone's attention that spring Sunday morning. There was a rather dim girl at the cash desk, and two men were working flat out around the ovens. He took out his ID and flashed it in the direction of the proprietor, a slim, worried-looking man in his fifties. He came over, visibly reluctant.

"We're very busy."

"I can see that. Is that Silvio?"

He nodded in the direction of the small, frantically busy young man who was constructing pizzas as if he was aiming at the Book of Records.

"No. Silvio is off today. That boy I have on loan from the Trattoria Aliberti."

"I see. You normally have two boys, don't you?"

"Yes. Is both off duty today."

"Ah. . . . Right. Well, I'll come round and hope to see him tomorrow."

Hesitantly, uncertainly, Signor Gabrielli said, "Of course. Yes. All right. I'll tell him."

Thoughtfully Charlie walked back to his car. He very much doubted that he was going to be talking to Silvio in the near future. It might be that some kind of alert would have to be put out, though they would need more hard evidence that there was a connection with the dead man. It could be, he thought, that they could use more subtle methods. He looked at his watch. One fifteen. Service at St Saviour's would be long over. However, he drove towards it and cruised along the road that it stood on. The church was a large Victorian construction, abounding in knobs and small spires. He had read a smart journalistic piece once saying how much better Victorian Gothic was than the real thing. He didn't think the author could have been thinking of St Saviour's.

He was just about to speed up towards the vicarage when he saw the door open at the Five Hundred pub, a short way away, and a family group emerge. He pulled his car up beside the kerb and watched them in the mirror as they came in his direction. It was the conventional enough family group — father, mother, daughter, daughter's boyfriend, son — yet somehow ill-assorted: or rather, with one discordant element, one cuckoo in the nest. The one whom he identified as the son seemed not to walk or talk or behave generally in the natural way the others had. It was as if he was conscious of being, or had persuaded himself that he was, on show.

Charlie got out of the car as they approached.

"Hello," he said to Rosemary.

"Hello." He was unsure how much welcome there was in the greeting. She turned to her family. "This is one of the detectives on the Mills case. I'm sorry, I've forgotten your name."

"DC Peace."

"Peace be with you," said the son, and let out a laugh like the last of the bathwater escaping. He laughed alone. Charlie behaved as people do when they have heard every possible joke on their name.

"This is Mark," said Rosemary, in a voice pregnant with meaning. "Janet and her boyfriend Kevin. And my husband Paul."

"I'll probably want to talk to all of you before long — me or my boss. It was just you I wanted to ask about something at the moment," he added, turning to Rosemary. She nodded, though Charlie felt she was suppressing anxiety. They let the others walk on, then followed at some distance behind.

"I'm trying to get something straight about the party last night," Charlie began. "You said you were behind the table that the food was to be served from, and Mills was one of a little group standing about nearby, right?"

"That's right."

"Tell me what happened when the food arrived."

"I thought I had done. Let me see. . . ." Rosemary's voice had been edgy. Now she put on an air of trying to visualise the scene. Charlie was sure that she had thought about it all too often since their earlier talk. "The deliveryman from Pizza Pronto came in, bang on the dot when we had arranged. He had a pile of pizzas up to his chin. He put them down in front of us on the table, then I and the other ladies each took one out of its carton and started cutting them up."

"And the deliveryman?"

"He left, of course."

"There was no . . . confrontation, episode of some kind, between him and Mills?"

"Not that I noticed. I was busy slicing pizzas. It's not that easy if they have a crispy bottom."

"There was no question of the man from

Pizza Pronto helping you?"

Rosemary made gestures of just having remembered.

"Ah — that's right. I'd forgotten that. I asked him if he'd like to help — him being so much quicker and better than us, probably — and he started round, then remembered they were very busy at the take-away and said he'd better not be away too long."

Rosemary was a guileless liar, Charlie decided, but hardly a wise one: she must surely realise that parish gossip about her and the Pizza Pronto boy would get to the police before long. Then a thought struck him: probably she was lying to give the boy time to get away. When she was sure he had, she would come clean. He could of course have challenged her version of events and of the situation, but he preferred to give the appearance of accepting it, if only on the well-worn principle of giving someone enough rope. He smiled down at her.

"Well, that clears that up," he said. They had finished up outside the vicarage. "Are you going to eat straight away? I wondered if I might pop in and have a word with your family. They were all at the party, weren't they?"

"Yes, they were. You won't want me, will

you? I've all sorts of little things to do in the kitchen."

The Sheffield family were assembled in the dining room, talking and laughing. They were apparently unconcerned by Mills's death, and by the reappearance of the policeman investigating it. When Charlie asked if they had talked to Mills at the party they all shook their heads.

"He was talking to local businessmen," said Paul Sheffield, who seemed, of them all, the most at ease. "He tended to. If there was no woman he was interested in, he liked to be polishing up his contacts."

"*De mortuis nil nisi bonum,*" said Mark. He considerately turned to Charlie and translated in a kindly tone. "One should only speak good of the dead."

"That would make murder investigations practically impossible," said Charlie.

"I've always thought that a silly injunction," said Paul. "Surely it should be while they're living that you shouldn't speak ill of people."

"So none of you had anything to do with him last night?" Charlie asked. He saw a flash of something pass over the daughter's eyes, but her boyfriend jumped in.

"I don't even know which one he was. It's very frustrating. Towards the end of the eve-

192

ning Janet introduced me to Mrs Harridance, and the rest of the time passed like a blur."

"I believe he's been a member of the St Saviour's congregation for some time," said Charlie, turning to Paul.

"Oh yes, quite a while. Since my time here, but it must be something like . . . oh, twelve years or more."

"Do you remember how or why he started coming?"

"I can't say. I suppose he'd just moved here — that is the usual reason." He paused, as his wife came into the room. "Do you remember how Dark Satanic — how Stephen Mills started coming to St Saviour's?"

His question had been drowned in a gale of laughter from his wife and daughter.

"Really, Father, you've given the policeman a totally false impression of the man!" protested Mark.

"Not so bloody false," muttered his sister.

"Right," said Rosemary, becoming businesslike again. "How did Dark Satanic Mills come to be a member of St Saviour's congregation? I've asked myself often enough why he was a member at all. . . . I somehow associate him with old Mr Unwin. That's his father-in-law. He was much spryer then, of course, and in complete control. I seem to think either he brought him along, or they were often together."

"He and Dorothy weren't married then, though," put in Paul. "And Mr Unwin wasn't a member of our church. He was a red-hot Evangelical. I married Stephen and Dorothy — what? — about ten or more years ago."

"I rather think that marriage to Dorothy sprang from his friendship with her father," said Rosemary. "Odd way round, that."

"You said to me that you didn't think Dorothy Mills was a very important element in Stephen Mills's life," said Charlie. "What was it that made you think that?"

"It was only an impression," said Rosemary thoughtfully. "It's just that you don't see them around together much. Oh, occasionally she'd come to church, or to one of our do's, but it was occasionally. If we were at a concert or the theatre in Leeds you might see Stephen, but to my recollection we hardly every saw him and his wife together."

"If you had to make any sort of date or arrangement with him," said her husband, "he'd take out his diary and consult it, but he'd never say he'd have to ask his wife. Most men do these days — as a sort of sop, I suppose — but he never did."

"And you implied there were other women," Charlie pressed him.

"That was certainly the impression given. I wouldn't be able to name any names."

Mark nodded wisely, as if his previous strictures had been justified. Charlie could imagine Mark being exceedingly irritating. He turned to Rosemary.

"Could you name any names?"

"No, I couldn't. You might say that if there weren't he should have been sued for false pretences. It was really a question of manner. He exuded confidence in his powers of attraction. If any woman gave the slightest sign of responding he was in there pressing his advantage home. But as to *evidence* of his sleeping with any of them — no, I'm afraid I have none."

"Isn't that odd?" Charlie asked.

"Maybe," said Rosemary, not seeming convinced. "But maybe he took care to keep that side of himself away from the congregation. I've certainly seen him emerging from a pretty sleazy massage parlour in town — The Sinful Sunbed, in Potter Street. He just grinned, quite unembarrassed. So perhaps he didn't want to compromise his position at St Saviour's."

"That suggests his position there was important to him," said Charlie.

"Though there's also the possibility that the ladies there are just not very tempting."

Once again Charlie could have sworn that a shadow passed over Rosemary's daughter's face.

# CHAPTER THIRTEEN

# *Partners*

On his way back to base Charlie dropped in at the flat he shared with his girlfriend Felicity. It was a one-bedroom affair, but with a large living room they had already made cheerful and personal by their own choice of pictures and bits and pieces of furniture. Felicity was surrounded by books and was hunched over a blank writing pad.

"So what made them summon you early?" she asked.

"It's a murder."

"It's lovely being a policeman's partner," commented Felicity. "You have such lovely casual conversations about perfectly horrible things."

"I'm surprised none of your ghoulish university friends have rung to tell you."

"They know I'm supposed to be writing an essay. Who was it?"

"Know a man called Stephen Mills?"

"Never heard of him."

"Ask around of your friends — particularly women."

"Particularly a certain sort of woman student, I suppose."

"Yes. . . . Felicity, you go to Pizza Pronto more often than I do."

"Don't I ever! All those nights when you say you'll be home and then ring to say you're working late."

"Would you recognise the boys who work there?"

She frowned, sidetracked.

"The boys? Is it all right to call them 'boys,' I wonder?"

"Spare me the intricacies of political correctness. Would you know them?"

"It's only recently that there's been two. I've only seen the new one once, and there was nothing very remarkable about him."

"And the other?"

"Oh yes, I've seen him often. The proprietor speaks to him in Italian, but I don't think he is. Maybe North African."

"Both the boys have scarpered, or so I suspect. The new one won't be in the Leeds area, if he knows what's good for him, but the other one may be. Neither of them has a work permit, if my guess is right."

"You're not harassing illegal immigrants, are you, Charlie?"

"In my job I do what I'm told to do," said Charlie impatiently. It was an old argument. "But no — the new one is involved somehow in the murder, and I'd like to know if he said anything to the other that might throw light on it. He's quite likely to have gone to some other pizzeria in town. Could you alert some of your student friends to look out for him?"

Felicity thought, then shook her head.

"I doubt that would work. He's probably gone to a quite different area of Leeds, hasn't he?"

"Probably."

"Students change digs, but they don't often move right across town. You hear of something going in your area and you snap it up. . . . Quite apart from the question of whether they *want* to help the police . . . Wouldn't it be better to drive around and look?"

"When we have a spare week, I suppose."

"It wouldn't take that long," said Felicity confidently. "I'll look in the Yellow Pages for likely places and map out a route. I could cruise around myself, just look through the windows. You won't need the car, I suppose?"

"I'll be working all the hours God sends,

and then some."

When Charlie got back to headquarters he was told that Oddie had just come in with a witness. He found them in a corridor on the way to an interview room and was introduced to Brian Ferrett. He was a chunky, slightly chubby young man, with thick brown curls framing a moonlike face and a manner that would have been encouraging on a school playing field — cheery, a little too loud. If he showed signs of nervousness, that was to be discounted; it was one of the most common reactions to murder, among the innocent as much as among the guilty.

"It's just incredible," he said to Charlie when they had been introduced. "Mind-blowing. I mean, you couldn't meet a more decent bloke than old Steve. And so full of life."

That was as of yesterday, Charlie felt like saying. But he held his peace and, with Oddie, ushered him through to the interview room.

When the formalities had been gone through, it was Oddie who started the questioning.

"You were Stephen Mills's — partner, was it? Or second in command?"

"Second in command," Ferrett said, readily and unresentfully. "Though he treated me more like a partner. I'd practically worked my way up from office boy."

"In how many years was that?"

"I'd been with him eight years. The business had been going nearly a year when he took me on."

"And I gather you do — you've been doing — a lot of the travelling involved in recent times."

"Yes, I do a lot of that. Stephen still had his places where he had a special expertise, good contacts he wanted to maintain. But yes — a lot of it I'd been getting to do, and developed my own contacts and expertise. Due off tomorrow, as a matter of fact —" He saw something in Oddie's face and said hurriedly, "Nothing that can't be put off."

"How did you come to get the job?"

He leaned back in his chair confidently.

"He wanted someone good with languages. It's something I've never found a problem. I graduated in Russian, but there were no jobs around. I had French and German as well, to Advanced level. Stephen saw that there was use for Russian in all the Eastern bloc countries where it was taught, and when he realised I was very fast at learning new languages he took me on. He was tremendously farsighted: he could see that things were loosening up in Eastern Europe. Hungary, Bulgaria, then gradually the rest — like the old domino theory in the Far East, only in reverse. Steve was just waiting for it to happen, then going in to see how he could help."

"Help?"

"Do business with them. That is helping them. We had what they need — taught them the skills they need."

"Is it in Eastern Europe where most of your business lies?"

"Oh no. But it's the *developing* part of our business. The bulk occurs in the Common Market countries. That's where the money is. In spite of all the processes of standardisation, each country has its peculiarities and quirks, its little hurdles you have to jump. It's those we can advise customers about, as well as putting them in touch with individual firms with marketing interests that coincide with their own."

"I see. And is business flourishing?"

"Oh yes!" he said, with positively boyish enthusiasm. "Brilliant. Of course we were hit by the recession, especially when it really started biting on the Continent as well. But we've weathered it — and now things are picking up in a big way."

It was the first time Charlie had heard anyone outside government claim that things were picking up.

"So you were both busy?"

"No question of that. Still, we're used to it. There was a time when Steve was running his father-in-law's business as well. That *really* took twenty-five hours a day!"

"Not much time for personal life, when you're working that hard," said Oddie neutrally. Ferrett shot him a glance, markedly less confident.

"Well, Steve was more or less only doing it as a favour to his wife's father."

"Somebody commented that Dorothy Mills was something of an irrelevance in her husband's life," put in Charlie. Brian Ferrett spread out his hands in a gesture of coming clean.

"Look, he was a bloke in a thousand. Straight as a die, old Steve. He'd never willingly have hurt Dottie. But maybe — and it *is* maybe, because we didn't discuss it — maybe he realised early on that he'd made the wrong choice. She's a nice enough lady, but she's got no class, to put it bluntly. She's not sexy or elegant, and she was no use at all in the business. Stephen was no monk. Maybe — again, maybe — he got what he wanted elsewhere. But he stayed with her, had her dad living with them, and I never heard him give her a cross word. Not every wife could say the same. Fair's fair. He did his duty to her."

It was a long speech, but Oddie didn't find it an entirely convincing one. He certainly didn't believe this was a subject they had never discussed.

"Where was the 'elsewhere' where he got what he needed?" asked Oddie. Ferrett shrugged.

"Search me. It wasn't something we talked about, like I said. I only know there were times when I didn't ask him where he'd been, know what I mean? My *impression* is that there may have been one or two affairs, but that mostly he got what he wanted by paying for it, if you get me."

"I get you," said Oddie with a man-to-man smile. "Now, obviously in this sort of enquiry we have to look for enemies of the dead man. Do you know of any?"

"Of course I've thought," said Ferrett, engagingly candid. "Thought all the way here. It's what first springs to mind, isn't it? But there's none I know of in his business life. Why should there be? He was providing a service, and there was nothing to speak of in the way of competition. He'd carved out his own little niche."

"Clever of him. What about dissatisfied customers?"

Ferrett shook his head confidently.

"It doesn't do to have dissatisfied customers. If there were any that felt they'd been given bad advice, or hadn't got their money's worth, Steve scrapped the bill or sent them a much smaller one. That was only sensible business practice."

"What about his earlier life?"

"Before he came to Leeds? I've no idea. Never discussed it. I think he came from London."

"But he never mentioned a father or mother? Or other family? Friends from the time before he came to Leeds?"

"Not to me. I've always had the impression that both parents were dead."

"Unusual for a man in his forties."

"Maybe. Could have been some kind of accident."

"Of course. But from all we've found out Mills seems to have emerged in Leeds like some kind of phoenix from the ashes."

"If you say so. By the time I met him he was already married to Dorothy and very much part of the family there. He and old Unwin were thick as . . . very close. It never occurred to me to ask about his earlier life."

For two people who had worked closely for years there seemed to be many subjects they had kept away from.

"We have to ask, though. *Some*where

there's got to be a motive for his murder."

"You don't think it could be sexual? That he was murdered by someone he picked up on the way home?"

Oddie shrugged.

"It's possible. Anything is possible, nothing is ruled out. But if you look at the pattern of that sort of crime you see that homosexuals are sometimes murdered by violent men they've picked up, prostitutes likewise. But a prostitute murdering a client? It may happen, but we'd want to find a pretty strong *other* reason, if you get my meaning."

"But if she wasn't a prostitute — say a student, and if he'd forced her . . ." Ferrett saw his mistake immediately. "But of course Steve wouldn't. It's inconceivable. Wouldn't have needed to, quite apart from anything else. And he wasn't that type at all, not at all."

He subsided, conscious of having put his foot in it. Charlie left a moment or two before he took up the questioning.

"Do you know of any connection between Mills and a young man who works in Pizza Pronto, on the Ilkley Road — he goes by the name of Silvio, but that probably isn't his real one."

Ferrett frowned.

"Never heard of him. Doesn't sound likely.

Our contacts are all with businessmen."

"What about the vicar of St Saviour's and his family?"

"Oh, he had lots to do with the Reverend Sheffield. They were both very active in Rotary. And of course old Steve threw himself into parish affairs."

"What about Sheffield's family? His daughter, for example?"

"Ah. . . . You mean did she have the hots for him?" Ferrett put on that all-males-together smile again. "There was a time when I thought so. We gave her a bit of typing to do at home, and after that she used that as an excuse for coming to the office whenever she could think of a reason."

"You don't know any more than that?"

"I don't. I've told you, that was an area of his life where I didn't ask questions. There may have been something going on. If so, it didn't last very long. She went off to college — oh, three years or more ago it must be now."

It was becoming clear that they weren't going to get any more out of Brian Ferrett for the time being. When they had shown him out of police headquarters Oddie and Peace turned and looked at each other.

"I don't —" they began simultaneously, then stopped.

"Trust him an inch?" suggested Charlie.

"Not a centimetre. All that 'straight as a die, old Steve' stuff. I never met Mills, but he was employing as his second in command a distinctly dodgy type."

"And if you take on and promote a dodgy type, the chances are you are a dodgy type yourself, and the business you're into is dodgy as well."

"A business that claims to be doing well at the moment has to be suspect."

"Especially one dealing with Europe, where everyone's in the doldrums."

"You don't trust the people close to Stephen Mills, do you?" Oddie said, looking at his sidekick. "You didn't trust his wife either, unless I'm mistaken."

Charlie considered.

"That was different. I didn't *believe* the wife. I might have trusted her on other matters, in other circumstances. There's no way I'd trust this joker on anything."

"The question is, what was the dodgy business they were both engaged in? And I have a mountain of paper that I'm going to have to go through to try to find out."

"What's the drill?" asked Charlie, without enthusiasm. "Do we sit down and go through it all together?"

"I thought about that. It has its advantages,

but it leaves the 'people' side of the case up in the air. Is there anyone we ought to be talking to now?"

"Ah . . . well, there's the Sheffield children. They seem to be up for the weekend, so we ought to talk to them as soon as possible. I had a hunch the girl knew something about Mills she wasn't letting on about, and now we've talked to Ferrett it's pretty obvious what it was."

"Yes," said Oddie slowly, adding a caution: "though Ferrett was all the time trying to shift our attention to his private life rather than his business affairs."

"Right. Even to suggesting that straight as a die old Steve was a rapist. But, whatever the dodgy business they were engaged in, the possibility is still there that he was killed because of something in his private life."

"Agreed. Anything else?"

"I'd like to track down the other boy who worked in the pizza place. My suspicion is that they've both gone missing but that the other one may still be in the Leeds area. If I'm right they were both working here illegally. If that is so, they'd have had a bond, they'd have talked."

"The priority is to get hold of the boy called Silvio."

"Of course it is. But what chance, with

no name and no photograph?"

"And Mrs Sheffield?"

"Is saying nothing. But there is one pos-sibility —"

"Yes?"

Charlie produced his idea without much hope.

"Bugging the Sheffield phone. I suspect he's fond of her and will contact her."

"Put it from your mind. You know it's out of the question."

Charlie shook his head regretfully.

"Any villain can walk into a shop and buy the latest hi-tech bugging device and a whole range of things for industrial espionage or any type of private spying. And we have to go to Home Secretary level."

"But those are the rules. We do. Any evidence we got would be useless if we'd done anything else."

"It wasn't so much evidence I wanted to get. Just where this young man *is*. I suppose the best we'll have to hope is that once the chap is well out of our reach Mrs Sheffield will come in and tell us what he told *her*. Whatever that is, it probably won't be much if he is fond of her and wants her to think well of him."

"Mike!" Somebody was bustling along with a piece of paper, and handed it over. It was a white-coated man from the mortuary. "Preliminary P.M. report."

Mike Oddie skimmed through it, then went back and read it through with more care.

"Well?" asked Charlie.

"Pretty much what we thought. He was attacked, beaten up — there's some evidence of martial arts techniques, maybe from someone who'd learnt a few blows, basic self-protection stuff. He was stunned, unconscious, when his throat was cut. They're not going to stick their necks out — *of course* they're not going to stick their necks out! — but they say it's possible he was unconscious for some time before his throat was cut."

"So, getting fanciful, one of the Sheffields could have beaten him up, gone home for the carving knife, then come back and done him in?"

"Theoretically. It's not a scenario I'd go for."

"I wasn't being serious. On the other hand, if you have a knife and want him dead, why not use it straight away?"

It was something they both pondered as they went their separate ways.

# CHAPTER FOURTEEN

# *Terrible Good Cause*

*C*harlie thought with satisfaction of the mountains of paper Mike Oddie had taken home with him to get to the bottom of Stephen Mills's business affairs. By the time he saw them they would have been filleted by an expert hand, and only the ones of possible relevance to the case would need to be read and pondered. All very much to the good. Charlie's interest in crime was people: faces, attitudes, gestures, signs of hidden woes and hidden passions. The intricacies of financial malpractice could interest him only when they led him to the mind that had conceived them.

And there were other ways of getting into contact with that mind, and other aspects of it that were to him of more interest. As soon as he got to his desk he looked at his watch. It was coming up to half past six. After a moment's thought he got out his telephone

212

directory and rang the Sheffields.

"Oh, Mrs Sheffield, it's DC Peace here. . . . Progressing, but a long way from concluded yet. I wondered, Mrs Sheffield, how long your children were going to be there."

"Oh, Mark is with us till tomorrow evening," Rosemary said, with no obvious signs of pleasure in her voice. "Janet and Kevin are driving back to London later tonight."

"Then I wonder if I could talk to Janet, please?"

"Of course."

There was a pause before she said it, the involuntary giveaway of someone not used to dealing with the police, then a longer pause before her daughter came on the line with a very tentative "Hello?"

"Hello, Miss Sheffield. This is DC Peace — we met earlier. I thought since you're leaving Leeds tonight we ought to talk about the party last night."

"Oh, should we? Is there any need? I've told you everything I know."

"It's perfectly normal," said Charlie, in his comfortable-copper voice, "just routine. You're the only person that I know of — you and your boyfriend — who'll be leaving Leeds. . . . And we need to talk about Stephen Mills generally."

"Oh." There was a silence of several sec-

213

onds, and then he detected a note of relief in her voice when she said, "Yes, I suppose we do. I think I'd prefer to come to you."

"Excellent. You'll know the Leeds Police Headquarters, of course. And could you bring — Kevin, is it? — with you?"

"Yes, I suppose so. . . . He doesn't know anything about Stephen Mills."

"Just a matter of routine, like I said," said Charlie smoothly. "I'll hope to see you in twenty minutes or so."

They arrived together at the desk, an appealing-looking couple, humorous and warm, with an air of suiting each other. Charlie thought he might have a lot in common with Kevin. But it wasn't Kevin that was of principal interest, and he resisted the suggestion that he should talk to them together.

"It's never done," he said. "But if you'll wait here, sir, I'll have a chat with you later."

It had been Kevin, not Janet, who suggested that he might talk to them together, and Charlie got the impression she felt a sort of relief that he had vetoed the proposal. Once in the interview room she sat forward in her chair opposite him with a nervous expectancy. She was not a beautiful girl, but she was healthy, sharp-eyed, alert. If the word "wholesome" had not been devalued, she would have been that.

Charlie came straight to the point.

"You knew Stephen Mills a lot better than you've been letting on, didn't you?"

"Yes. Who told you, I wonder? Was it that awful Ferrett person? Oh, never mind. Yes, I did know him better than I've been letting on."

"And a lot better than your mother realises, I would guess."

"Yes, mother never knew anything beyond the fact I'd done some secretarial work for the firm. I'd be glad if you didn't have to tell her now."

"I don't see why I should need to."

"Good. She loathed him. Somehow I'd feel . . . devalued in her eyes if she found out. In our house he was always 'Dark Satanic Mills' — an object of suspicion, though I don't think they ever made up their minds what they suspected him of. I think that probably made him more attractive in my eyes — the Byronic man of mystery, the attractive rotter, that kind of thing."

"Did he turn out like that on closer acquaintance?"

She frowned.

"You know, in one way he *did*. In the sense that he must have *had* a past, like the Byronic hero, but I never found out anything about it beyond dark hints. For example, his speech was very precise, almost old-fashioned, but it told you nothing about where he came from."

"Did you find out what he did?"

She looked surprised.

"Yes, of course. I thought you must have found out about me from Brian Ferrett. I did typing work for Stephen. His business was facilitating the work of exporters, particularly in Europe — finding markets for people, getting things through all the red tape, making contact for them with people who mattered."

"And that was all the company did?"

"So far as I know. . . ." She pondered. "I was hardly at the heart of the business, but all the typing I did for him and Brian was about things like that."

"I suppose it would have been. But your relationship wasn't just boss-typist, was it?"

"No," said Janet flatly. "I threw myself at him, to tell you the truth. Quietly, in private — so there was no scandal. I went through a long phase, I suppose it was a kind of prolonged adolescence, of finding dark, Latin, rather oily men attractive. The Valentino type. They all turned out to be rather awful. When they made love they were really making love to themselves. Mills was one of a line."

"And he was no exception, I suppose."

"No. If anything an intensification of the tendency."

"Where did you go?"

"To make love? All sorts of places. Sometimes in the open air — Ilkley Moor, or on the Haworth–Hebden Bridge moors. This was summer, and there were lots of hot days."

Charlie racked his brains to remember the last hot summer, but failed.

"When would this have been?"

"Five years ago."

"But when it wasn't hot?"

"He had a flat — a small, rather insalubrious little place over a shop in the Ilkley Road."

"What kind of shop?"

"A camera shop — Snaps was the name."

"Was it just a flat to take girls to?"

"So far as I know. When we went there I felt as if I was one of a long line and was part of a routine."

She made no effort to keep the distaste and self-loathing out of her voice.

"No signs of business done from there?"

"No. But I wasn't there much — a quick in and out, you might say."

"How long did the affair last?"

"Oh, five or six weeks. The length of the school holidays."

"You were still at school?"

"Yes, coming up to my last year."

"How did it start?"

"Well, I fancied him. Quite shamelessly, I'm afraid. So as I said, I threw myself at him. To that extent he was blameless. After church one Sunday I went up to him and asked him if he had any typing or computer work I could do in the holidays. I could see in his eyes that he had something in mind other than typing and that he knew I had too. Humiliating to look back on."

"So he agreed, and it went on from there."

"Yes. He gave me some work, bedded me, and I kept on going back on the excuse of wanting more work if it was going. I hate myself for it now."

"Everyone has one or two big mistakes in that line."

"I had a whole series."

"How did it end? Did you just go back to school?"

"Not quite. No, that wouldn't have ended it. . . ." She thought before she spoke, making Charlie very aware that this was the most difficult part. "I had had the feeling for some time that he was getting bored. If I'd had any savvy I'd have cooled it, played hard to get, but I was very immature. I kept going round there, supposedly to see if he had any jobs, but in reality . . . well, I suppose I don't need to spell it out. Anyway one day he said 'OK, there's a job for you, but we'll have to fetch it.' So we got into the car and drove to this large house —"

"In Abbingley?"

"Oh yes. Not far. And he opened the front door with his own key, and I was just realising it was his own house when he took me into the sitting room and introduced me — no, it was more like he was flaunting me — to his wife. He said: 'Hello, Dottie. You know Janet, don't you? She's come round to do something for me.' And he . . . he *leered*. And before I knew what he was doing he took me upstairs and into a big double bedroom that I imagine was his and hers, or had been once, and he was stripping off, and stripping me as well and . . . well, I suppose I don't have to go on."

"You didn't resist?"

She stared down at the table, remembering.

"I did . . . but very feebly. Just said things like, 'Stephen, we can't.' Quite useless, really. It was as if he had some kind of *power*. I suppose girls have said that from time immemorial. I think because I was so young and knew so little, and he was so mature and worldly-wise and — *corrupt,* that there was a kind of power he had over me and enjoyed. It was like being mesmerised by a snake."

"You think his wife knew what you were doing?"

"Oh, of course she knew, and that was the point."

"How did she look when he took you to meet her?"

"Oh, it's difficult to describe. Weary. Almost indifferent."

"Was there hate there?"

"Maybe. But she didn't show it. She didn't even show contempt for me, if she felt it. Her look was more . . . pitying."

"Did you see her again?"

"No. When we'd done he just got up and put his clothes on, and I did the same. Back to business seemed to be the message he wanted to get across. On the way out, in the hall, we met the father — old 'Onions' Unwin, her father. Stephen said, 'Oh, you know Janet Sheffield, don't you, Dad? Paul and Rosemary's girl. She's been doing work for us at the shop.' The old chap sort of bumbled a greeting, Stephen shouted ' 'Bye, Dottie,' and we left the house. He was oozing with self-satisfaction. He drove me home, hardly speaking, but he gave a nasty grin as he dropped me off at the vicarage as if the fact that I was the vicar's daughter gave added spice — maybe the only spice — to the affair. That was his sort of humour."

"And — ?" asked Charlie.

"And that put paid to it. I suppose that was the intention. Nobody was in, and I went up to my room and sobbed and sobbed. You know people nowadays are always talking about low self-esteem? That was the rock bottom of my self-esteem. I bathed him out of me, and by the time I had finished I knew that the affair was over, knew that I wanted it to be over, and knew that I would never ever look at that type again."

"Have you seen much of him since?"

"I've *seen* him often enough. Couldn't avoid that, with him always being at church. I've not exchanged a word until last night at the party. He came up behind me and whispered, 'How come we never get together these days?' I gave him a look and froze him out. I think he only came up because he saw I had a boyfriend and was happy with him. That would have been something worth ruining. And I knew he really hated women who rejected him or showed him that he could never get anywhere with them. It's not very effective after he definitely *has* got somewhere with them, but that's why I froze him out."

"So the fascination had really worn off."

"Really!" She looked him in the eye with

what seemed a genuine frankness. "It had become repulsion. But that summer it was like a basilisk. It was only the sheer nastiness and cruelty of what he did and made me an accomplice in doing that saved me."

"What did you feel when you heard he was dead?"

"Nothing. I'm glad I didn't feel exultation, feel my humiliation had been revenged or anything melodramatic like that. I was empty of feeling for him."

"Could you have killed him yourself?"

She thought.

"No. I suppose you'll think, 'She would say that,' but since you thought it worth asking, I'll tell you. I couldn't have killed him, not even *then*. I felt disgust for myself, and I think that's what I felt for him too. Disgust, not hatred."

"Do you think that's what his wife felt as well?"

"I couldn't fathom what she thought then. She's the sort you look at and feel you never can. Those eyes — they're almost frightening. I think the old phrase about still waters running deep very much applies there."

Charlie shifted in his chair.

"The emotions you feel towards Mills are pretty similar to the ones your mother feels towards him, aren't they?"

"I suppose so. I've come to toe the family line on the subject."

"Do you think your mother could ever have had a similar experience?"

Her eyes opened wide.

"*No!* No, I really don't. I never thought about it, but it's absolutely out of the question. Mother and father are completely faithful to each other."

"A lot of children feel that about their parents, quite wrongly. And there has been talk in the parish recently about your mother and the boy from the pizzeria."

"Oh, you're on to that, are you?"

"I haven't talked about it with your mother yet. Have you?"

Janet nodded.

"A little. She is fond of him, she is sorry for him, she wanted to help him. Anyone would feel the same, except for someone like that old battle-axe Florrie Harridance. That's *all* there was to it. No affair. And no affair with Stephen Mills either."

"You're very loyal. Do you think your brother feels the same?"

"Mark? Oh, he's training for the priesthood and knows nothing whatever about real life."

"He struck me as a pillock."

"He is. You wouldn't trust his opinion rather than mine, would you?"

"No, I wouldn't," said Charlie truthfully. Especially as on the whole Janet's agreed with his own.

Janet's boyfriend Kevin had little to tell. He admitted that he had spent most of the evening observing the wrong things — in his case Mark Sheffield and Florrie Harridance. He had been watching and listening to them with an inexorable author's interest, and anything else had passed him by.

When he had got rid of them both it was half past nine. Time to knock off for the day. Charlie made some notes to himself for the next day's work and then drove back to the flat. His plans for a cosy supper and an early night were shattered the moment he opened the door.

"Do you want him?" Felicity asked.

"Who?"

"The boy from Pizza Pronto — the other one. I could be mistaken because he was working at the back of a long, narrow takeaway place, but I think he's at Pizza Suprema, which is on the Crompton Road — number 45."

Charlie thought, looking round regretfully.

"If I don't get him now — " he said, and then turned and ran down the stairs again. Felicity knew better than to ask if she could come. She felt rather proud, however, of the participation she had been allowed thus far and knew that that wasn't something Charlie was going to mention to Mike Oddie.

Charlie spotted Pizza Suprema well before he got there, so he parked a good way away. It was on a corner, and the little yard at the back was open to the street. He sauntered towards the place. The back door was open, and the lid of a garbage bin was on the ground. The boy — *a* boy — was cleaning up for the night. When he reached the place Charlie nipped into the shadows of the yard and waited. It was only a couple of minutes before the young man came out with an armful of tins, packets and other debris and began piling them into the bin. When he banged the lid on it and turned to go in he found Charlie in the doorway.

"Before you do anything silly, like trying to run away," Charlie said, "let's get this straight: I am a policeman but I'm not in the least interested in seeing your papers. I don't care if you're on the run from the police of five continents and I certainly don't care if you're working here illegally."

The young man was coffee-cream-coloured, round-faced and curly-haired. He looked at Charlie uncertainly.

"*C'est Stanko, n'est-ce-pas?*" he said, then

changed to a very Gallic English. "It is about Stanko, is it not?"

"If he's the one who's sometimes called Silvio, yes. Shall we go inside?"

He stood aside, and they went into a long, narrow kitchen still smelling irresistibly of tomatoes and garlic and basil and oregano. He was reminded that he had had nothing but a sandwich all day. The young man, with the instinct of the hotel trade, sensed his need.

"You 'ave 'unger? You like 'alf a pizza?"

Charlie nodded, just at the moment when his stomach let out a pathetic whine. The boy smiled, took a large pizza from a cooling oven and cut it in half. When he handed Charlie his section they both agreed to dispense with a knife and fork, biting into the gooey heart of the pie.

"You eat with me. You can't mean me 'arm," said the boy.

Charlie could think of colleagues who could share a pizza with a suspect and nick him while he was wiping his fingers, but he didn't mention them.

"What's your name?" he asked, and then amended that to "What shall I call you?"

"Call me Yussef," the young man replied.

"Right, Yussef. I'm not going to ask you anything about yourself. How long have you known — Stanko, is it?"

"Yes, Stanko. But I don't think that's 'is real name. 'E 'ave many names. 'E came about three weeks ago to Pizza Pronto."

"Did you get on well with him?"

"Yes, very well. 'E is a nice, gentle man, very *sympathique*. We talk a lot, 'ave a lot in common — you know?"

"I know. Where was he from?"

Yussef considered his loyalties before replying.

"'E is from Yugoslavia — what used to be Yugoslavia."

"Are you both Moslem?"

Yussef spread out his hands.

"We 'ave not discussed. I am Moslem, but not so much. If 'e is Moslem, I think 'e is even less."

"Right. Did he have any friends in Leeds?"

"Oh yes. 'E 'ave Mr and Mrs Sheffield, especially Mrs."

"Nobody else?" Yussef shook his head. "Or enemies?" Yussef shook his head again.

"Right, now about yesterday. Was it a normal day, or did anything stand out?"

The young man thought long before replying.

"The evening 'e was different. When 'e came down 'e was all shook."

"Shook?"

"Like 'e'd 'ad bad news, or 'ear something 'orrible."

"You say came down. You were in the takeaway?"

"Yes. One of us always prepare for the evening with Signor Gabrielli. The other came down when we opened at half past five. Stanko came down then, and 'e was all shook."

"Did he say why?"

"No. I asked and 'e shook 'is 'ead and said 'e didn't want to talk, but 'e would tell me later. Said it was *atroce*. We talk French and sometimes Italian together."

"What does it mean?"

" 'Orrible. Like you say a-att-atro-cee-us."

"Was that all he said?"

"Yes. 'E made a phone call — quite short. I didn't 'ear nothing what was said. We was very busy with lots of pizzas for the party at the church."

"He took them, didn't he?"

"Yes. 'E drove our little van."

"What about when he came back?"

"Was shook. Still more shook."

"I see. And what happened as the evening went on?"

"We was not so busy. About five to ten Stanko asked if 'e could go. Said 'e 'ad to meet someone. Signor Gabrielli said

228

'fine,' and 'e went."

"But that wasn't the last you saw of him?"

Yussef seemed to consider his loyalties again, then realised his own peril and shook his head.

"No. 'E come in about eleven, when I was going to bed. Come into my room, all very shook and upset. Said 'e 'ad to leave Leeds that night."

"Did he say why?"

"Said 'e 'ad been in a fight. 'E 'ad some martial hearts — said they was very useful in Yugoslavia, with lots of troubles even before the war start. 'E said 'e'd done awful damages to this man. 'E didn't think the man — 'e didn't say 'is name — would go to the police, but 'e couldn't risk it. Someone might find 'im before 'e come round, and call the police. So 'e 'ad to go."

"I see. And next day you heard of the murder?"

Yussef looked at him challengingly.

"'E is not a murderer. Is not possible. 'E is a *gentle* boy. But Signor Gabrielli, 'e think: better if neither of us is there, in case the police come, so 'e arrange a swap for me."

"With someone who has got his papers? Right. Stanko had already taken off, I suppose. Was there anything else — anything you know about Stanko?"

The young man shook his head.

"His surname?"

"We didn't ask. It was better."

"So you've nothing else to tell me?"

The boy came up close, wiping the tomato from his lips.

"Stanko is gentle. A good, gentle, peace-loving boy."

"A gentle boy with skills in martial arts?"

"Yes. That is the point of martial hearts. They protect you. Like they are taught to women who 'ave not great strength so they can protect themselves."

"And do you think Stanko was protecting himself last night?"

The boy looked down.

"I do not know. But if 'e attacked, 'e 'ad good cause. Terrible good cause."

## CHAPTER FIFTEEN

# *Talking About Rosemary*

*F*ascinating evening?" Charlie asked Mike Oddie when they came in to work next morning.

"Wonderful," said his boss. "Now I know what it's like to be drowned in paper."

"So you know all about his cash flow, his assets and liabilities, his business plan and whatever."

"I have an idea," said Oddie cautiously. "That is if his papers are an honest record. It all seems above board, it all seems like a genuine service which fills a real need. Letters testify that he had expertise and contacts, used them intelligently . . ."

"But?"

"But why do I get the idea that I know everything about his business except the most important thing?" He paused to sort his ideas out. "The only obvious 'but' is that I can't see from the records that it would have been all that profitable. Of course we don't know that Mills had a lavish life style, his wife probably has plenty of money, and yet —"

"And yet what we know of Mills doesn't suggest he'd be content with a modestly successful business."

"No, it doesn't," agreed Oddie enthusiastically. "That's not my picture, anyway."

"Was there anything to suggest other activities — any other source of income?"

"Well, only something very small, something I very nearly didn't pick up: there were a couple of references in business letters to 'number 94.' " He frowned, trying to be as exact as possible. "Quoting from memory they were: 'This is straying in the direction of number 94 matters' and 'I'll leave the unfinished number 94 business until I see you at Rotary.' Not a lot to go on."

"You don't want to ask the people who wrote the letters?"

"Certainly not now. I may have to as a last resort. If we assume it's an address, and if we start on the idea that it's in the Abbingley area of Leeds, there aren't a great many roads that go up as high as number 94."

"You could try a camera shop called Snaps," said Charlie reaching across the desk for the telephone directory.

"Why there?"

"It's to a flat above that he took Janet Sheffield. She saw it as a love nest, but it could have had a business side as well. Yes — here we are: Snaps, 94 Ilkley Road."

Oddie rubbed his hands.

"Right! Got it in one! Let's hear about your evening before we do anything more."

When he had heard Charlie's account of the two interviews, Oddie said: "What do you make of Stanko coming down at half past five in a foul mood?"

"I'm kicking myself I didn't ask Yussef what there was upstairs," Charlie admitted. "Was there a telephone? A television? Somehow or other he'd heard something that enraged him. That's how I read it, anyway."

"Why not ring Gabrielli at Pizza Pronto?"

Charlie leafed through the book and did just that. Luckily he found him in, taking in supplies. He also found him terribly and earnestly anxious to help the police. Charlie managed the conversation without even mentioning Stanko, and when he put the phone down he said: "Television but not telephone. If they needed to ring anyone they had to use the phone in the takeaway."

"So this 'Yussef' had been downstairs preparing for the evening trade, while Stanko was upstairs. It's a fair bet he wasn't watching *Neighbours* or *Home and Away*."

"It was Saturday, remember. The likely thing is the BBC news, which is generally just after five."

Oddie nodded.

"In his situation, coming from Yugoslavia, watching the news would be pretty obsessive, I'd guess. Get on to BBC North and see if you can get a video, and if not get on to Television Centre in London. I'll see about getting a warrant to search the flat above Snaps. Do you want to come along with me? Or have you got things to do on your own?"

As Oddie knew he would, Charlie said he had one or two things he'd like to do on his own, follow-up things. Charlie believed in hunting solo whenever possible. His first port of call was a shop called Flowers First. It was on University Road, and the name meant (as its proprietor Florrie Harridance would explain when asked or if unasked) that if couples had had a tiff they should buy flowers first and have the explanations afterwards. This certainly made commercial sense, and perhaps psychological sense as well. Whether the university people who largely lived in the Abbingley area were particularly liable to tiffs and makeups she did not say, but there were no signs of the shop being other than a viable financial concern when he dropped in there, other than the fact that there were no customers, which on a Monday morning was hardly surprising.

"We've not met, but we've spoken on the telephone," said Mrs Harridance, coming weightily forward like an aircraft carrier doing a manoeuvre in shallow water. "And I've caught a look at you as you've gone past in the police car."

"I stand out," agreed Charlie.

"You do. Footballers you expect, and pop stars and newsreaders and drug traffickers, but black policemen you notice, and you're the first that's come my way. Not that I have a lot to do with the police, though I've supplied flowers to funerals you've had an interest in, that's for sure."

Charlie murmured his interest.

"Well, it's the Mills murder you'll be wanting to talk about, won't you? Well, like I say, I'm not one to get involved with the police, and at St Saviour's —"

"Questions," said Charlie forcefully. "And answers."

"I beg your pardon, young man?"

"Questions and answers. I don't want to *talk about* anything. I want to ask questions, and get answers from you. Short and direct answers, please. Right?"

Florrie looked daggers, but nodded.

"Why was there all this fuss about Mrs Sheffield and the Mothers' Union?"

Florrie swallowed. Her answer, when it came, was more a protest against his demand for brevity than compliance with it.

"She lost her faith. The Mothers' Union is a church organisation. Everyone felt it wasn't right her holding office."

"I see," said Charlie carefully. "I can see that loss of faith would be fatal for a clergyman, but for his wife? You say 'everyone,' but I haven't come across a great deal of opposition to Mrs Sheffield as yet."

"Well of course it's not *personal*. It's a matter of principle. I mean we're all sorry for her (though I think she could make an *effort* to get it back) but when she's one of the officials of the organisation, and it's the main women's group in the parish —"

"Short," said Charlie. "Short answers. I get your point. But I'm not convinced it hasn't been a question of other people wanting to take over her job."

"You're trying to make it sound unpleasant, young man, but you'll not rile me. I'm made of sterner stuff. People who do jobs like chairing the Mothers' Union get no thanks for it, and no financial rewards either — not like the Masons and Rotarians. All you get is hard work from morning to night. So just because some people in the parish desperately wanted me to take over the chair, I'll not have you saying —"

"Right, well let's change the subject a bit. I gather that at some stage the matter developed into gossip about Mrs Sheffield's private life. Were you responsible for that?"

"I was *not*. Quite the reverse, young man, if you did but know. Not that I need to justify myself to you, but when Selena came to me with what she'd heard people saying in that guesthouse in Scarborough, I said 'Hold on,' I said. 'It's all very flimsy,' I said, 'and the last thing we'd want people saying about us is that we'd been spreading malicious gossip, and it could rebound on us,' I said —"

"Us?"

"Well —" She was caught up short. Charlie was sorry he had tried to insist on short answers, because she obviously gave more away when given her rein. "Well, I meant those of us who thought it was time for a change, and time for those who'd been occupying all these positions for years to step aside and let others have the chance."

Charlie was a mite puzzled by this, because there was a ring of truth about what she said, and an atom of shrewdness. There had always been, he suspected, a good chance that sexual scandal about the vicar's wife, if ill-substantiated, would rebound on the scandalmonger. Apparently Mrs Harridance had recognised this.

"And yet the scandal did get around," he pointed out.

"Well eventually it did, yes. Don't ask me how. People only started gossiping later, more than a week after Selena got home from Scarborough, and it wasn't with my agreement, because I'd told her right away I thought it was wrong and silly. But then maybe she'd been talking to someone else, getting other advice —"

"Such as?"

A cunning look came into her bulging eyes.

"You'd better ask her that. I wouldn't know anything about Selena's private life. We're different generations. Manners are different these days, to say nothing of morals. Any road, she found she had to go round afterwards and take it all back, so it rebounded on us, like I said it would. I'm disappointed in Selena. Whoever gave her the advice, you couldn't say it was *good* advice, could you? Now what you'd best do, young man, and I'm sure you don't want my advice but you could do worse than take it, is go round to Selena's and ask her what and who —"

"That's exactly what I'll do," said Charlie and turned and got out of the shop.

As he drove to Selena Meadowes's house he was turning over in his mind two thoughts: if Florrie Harridance was to be believed, she and Selena had rejected using the Rosemary–Stanko story against her, believing it might do them harm rather than good. But later something had changed Selena's mind and she had gone ahead and used it. Secondly, Florrie knew, or had a good idea, what or who that was, but she wanted it to come from her lieutenant, especially since she felt let down by her. If these propositions were correct, they could be useful.

Selena Meadowes's reception of him was very different from Florrie Harridance's. The moment she opened the door to him her manner was winsomely welcoming to the point of flirtatiousness. She made no bones about the fact that she knew who he was, though Charlie had no idea which of his various activities of the day before she had watched him at. Perhaps the mere fact that he was black made her land on the right assumption. In any case she led him through to the sitting room and prepared — or so it seemed, and Charlie reserved judgment on that — almost enthusiastically to be grilled.

"Though to be honest I can't tell you much," she said, turning her full face and smiling a Doris Day smile, "because I wasn't that close to the Encounter."

"Encounter?"

"Between the boy from the pizza place and Stephen Mills of course!" she said, as if talking to a child. "That's what everyone is talking about, isn't it? I could see there was *some*thing — I mean, I could feel the tension, almost *see* the electricity in the air — but I was too far away to know what was going on. Luckily Derek was near."

"Is that your husband? I'll have to talk to him."

"Oh, he'll be *thrilled*. He says the moment Silvio saw Mills — he was on his way round to help dish out the pizzas — he was thunderstruck. Flabbergasted. Obviously there was *some*thing in that boy's past — something criminal Derek thought — that he had thought was hidden forever, and there was Stephen Mills who knew all about it."

"That's how it struck him, did it?"

"Oh, I think it struck everyone like that."

Charlie raised his eyebrows.

"Because it could be exactly the other way round, couldn't it? Something criminal or disgraceful in Mills's past that the boy knew about."

She screwed up her English rose forehead. "But why would he be thunderstruck?"

"Because he, or people close to him, had been affected by whatever criminal or disgraceful thing it was."

"Oh, I don't think that's very convincing. I don't want to teach you your job, but I mean, we've known Stephen at St Saviour's for *yonks*. And the boy is quite young."

"What about something disgraceful in his *present* life?"

"I don't think so," she said obstinately. "We know him."

She tried to give it a Lady Bracknell–like imprimatur of respectability.

"So what does your husband say happened then?"

"Silvio — if that is his name — turned, muttered something, some lame excuse or other, and fled. End of episode."

"I see," said Charlie neutrally. "Well, as I say, I'll have to talk to your husband if that episode does turn out to be significant. But that wasn't what I came to ask you about."

"Oh?" Slight access of tension, Charlie thought.

"It's the matter of Rosemary Sheffield I

wanted to talk about."

She smiled forgivingly.

"Rosemary? Oh, the whole parish knows about that. Rosemary lost her faith — quite suddenly, like mislaying your spectacles, or so it seems. Odd, isn't it? Everyone thought it so sad in a vicar's wife. *Awfully* embarrassing for both of them of course. But I can't see why you'd want to talk to me about *that*."

"Can't you? Well, let's just go through what happened after she lost her faith, can we? There was some trouble over the positions she holds, wasn't there?"

She bridled, very prettily.

"Well, where they were *church* positions there was bound to be, wasn't there? I mean, in a way she had signed herself *out* of the Church. So naturally people felt she shouldn't go on holding the positions she had had."

Charlie nodded, still very friendly. Those who knew him could have told Selena to beware.

"As I understand it, someone was retiring as chair of the Mothers' Union, and people — or rather *some* people, some parish members — didn't want Mrs Sheffield to move up from vice-chair and didn't want her to stay in that position. Is that a fair summary?"

"I suppose so, though you make it sound so nasty."

"I'm sorry. And Mrs Harridance would have liked to take over, is that right? And perhaps have you as her deputy?"

"Certainly there were some that wanted that — quite a *lot*, actually. But there was no row. I remember talking it over quite happily with Rosemary in the train when she was on her way back from Scarborough."

"Ah — I hadn't heard about that. Was that when you decided to go to Scarborough yourself?"

A shade came over her vapid prettiness.

"Well, no . . . No, I think that was later. I remember meeting Rosemary by chance in the street and asking her where she'd stayed, and thinking that was just the place to take my old mum, who needed a tonic."

"She must have recommended it powerfully. And while you were there, you met the boy who later came to work at Pizza Pronto and who confronted Stephen Mills at the church party?"

She pouted, not very prettily.

"You say 'met,' as if it was a social thing. Actually he was the waiter there."

"I know he was. And while you were there you heard a juicy story: that he had been

243

seen coming out of Mrs Sheffield's bedroom at night."

"Of course I never imagined —"

"And the day you left you heard he'd been sacked."

"We met the boy at the station, checking ticket prices, and that's what he told us. We were so sad."

"Right. Now we get to the interesting bit. You didn't use any of this when you got back to Leeds because you and Mrs Harridance thought that it might boomerang."

"That's most unfair!" said Selena, getting hot and flustered. "I would *never* have hurt Rosemary, who's the *sweetest* person. Who have you been talking to?"

"That's neither here nor there."

"I'll never speak to Florrie again!"

"What interests me is that something changed your mind. When you'd been home a week or so, the rumours started getting around. What was it made you switch tactics?"

"Nothing! I never spread those stories. If Florrie has told you so, she's lying."

Charlie leaned forward so his face was close to hers.

"I'm not sure you should try to pin blame on Mrs Harridance. I think you changed tactic because of someone else — someone you told the story to." Suddenly he saw a purple blush spreading up from her neck, and he added softly, just as speculation: "Pillow talk, perhaps?"

She broke down at once, taking out a delicate little hankie and a bundle of paper tissues and sobbing into the clumsy, absorbent ball, murmuring things like "You won't tell?" and "Derek would never forgive me." Charlie wished he could rid himself of the idea that he was being watched out of the corner of her eye and his reactions estimated. He congratulated himself on the success of his long shot, but he was in no mood to let Selena Meadowes off the hook. He said briskly:

"There's no reason why anyone should know if you are totally honest. How did Stephen Mills get to hear about this?"

"Well, I don't *know* — because we haven't talked about it, how could we? — but I gave my husband some little . . . well, *hints* about Rosemary and the waiter, and that evening he was going to Rotary, and I think —"

"I get the message. Coy little jokes about the vicar's wife having been a naughty girl. I was once told that men make the best gossips, and my experience is that it's true. What makes you think that was how it was?"

"The next day we met — Stephen happened to be around when I dropped the children at school. He'd never been there at that time before. And he was very . . . par*ti*cular. Very warm. And he'd never done more than freeze me before, or sneer, even though I'd . . . well, sort of . . ."

"You'd sent out signals and he hadn't responded?"

"That's a horrible way of putting it," she protested. "You . . . people are so crude."

Charlie grinned, his teeth glinting terrifyingly.

"Well then, you'd sent out tiny, ever-so-subtle hints indicating interest, and he pretended he hadn't registered them."

"No. He indicated he had registered them but wasn't interested. I've known him do that to others too."

"Whereas now, suddenly, he was all over you. *Where* was he all over you?"

"Oh really — you are so . . . He rang that evening, when he knew Derek would be watching the European Cup. Said he'd be at the Quality Inn in Leeds all day the next day, under the name of Cameron Winchell. If I'd care to come along to do secretarial work I'd be very welcome. I could use the name Beryl Bates. . . . I should have been outraged, or pretended to be, but . . ."

"You went along."

Her voice took on a whining tone.

"I was flattered, and . . . it's a terribly expensive hotel. Way outside our range. I told the receptionist I was there for secretarial work, like he'd said. . . . We were there from half past ten to when I had to pick the kiddies up from school. He gave me a wonderful time. He had a suite, and we ate lunch there, and we . . . But after lunch he started asking about Rosemary Sheffield."

"And you told him all you'd learnt at Scarborough?"

"Yes. It didn't seem to matter, somehow, him being a man. And we were in bed, and it was just — well, like you said, pillow talk. But then, when he'd got it all out of me, I was about to swear him to silence —"

"A bit late, though I don't suppose earlier would have made any difference."

There was silence, then she said in a tiny voice:

"I don't think it would. Because before I could say anything, he lay there and said, 'Very interesting. I owe Rosemary one.' And I got panicky and said, 'What do you mean? You're not to say anything,' and I went on a bit, and he turned to me and smiled and said, 'I never let a debt go unpaid. You should remember that. If someone's done me an injury, I do them one back. That's nature's law.' Then he got up and dressed and told me to do the same."

"End of perfect romance."

The unlovely pout returned to her lips.

"You're horrible . . . but so was *it,* really. The experience. He made it so clear that he'd got what he wanted, which wasn't even *me,* and that was the end of it. He really liked turning the knife, you know. As we were leaving the hotel, in the foyer and before we got to the door, he said, 'Good-bye Selena, see you around,' and waved — he did it then so the receptionist would hear. I felt about two feet tall."

"If he liked turning the knife," said Charlie, getting up, "and we've other evidence that he did, maybe it's not surprising that someone took a knife to him."

"It wasn't me!" said Selena eagerly. "I wouldn't have — I mean it was just an episode. But I was terrified Derek would find out. He would have —"

She stopped, a horrified expression on her face.

"Don't worry," said Charlie. "Regularly in a murder investigation we hear someone say that someone else would have killed if they'd known. It's just an expression."

Selena nodded. Encouraged, she made a last attempt to make a better impression.

"I wish you'd understand about . . . what

happened — my side of it, anyway. I *did* find him terribly attractive, had done for ages. I knew I was being unfaithful to Derek, of *course* I did, but somehow his showing interest was like a fairy tale, an Audrey Hepburn film come true, and it didn't seem sordid, or mean, but somehow . . . beautiful. I wish I could make you see that."

"I'll try," said Charlie. "But we blacks are so crude."

# CHAPTER SIXTEEN

# *Scenarios*

*Y*ou've got a nice new room for your little business," said the desk sergeant when Charlie arrived back at headquarters. "Very cosy — I think you'll like it. It's a sort of miniature United Nations in there."

Charlie saw what he meant when he'd been told where the room was and opened the door. Oddie had managed to get six small desks into a medium-sized room, and at them sat six people of various ages and types dictating translations of documents on to tape recorders in a variety of accents.

"And even so we've got two languages we haven't found translators for yet," said Oddie. "Azeri and Albanian. I'm not too worried. I'm getting the general picture."

"I'm glad about that," said Charlie, sitting on the edge of a desk. "And what is the general picture?"

"Settle down and I'll give it to you. . . . Number 94 was the centre of the other side of Mills's European activities — as well as a love nest, as we know. It's a two-bedroom flat, and most of this stuff was tucked away in filing cabinets in the second bedroom. He was good and methodical, thank heavens, so that's made the job easier. It's clear that the whole business grew into illegality, so to speak — left the track gradually before taking off into rough country. What started as a perfectly legitimate part of European Opportunities Ltd. began wobbling over during the eighties into something slightly off-colour, first, and then to something absolutely out of order."

"During the eighties . . . Was this because of some of the Balkan countries breaking free of the Soviet Union?" Charlie asked.

"Partly. But the biggest single factor was the rise of gangsterism in the Soviet Union itself. This started with bootlegging when Gorbachev tried to curb vodka consumption — a pretty futile endeavour, by the sound of it. Really it was very much like America during prohibition. Soon the bootlegging snowballed into large-scale crime and profiteering, with rival gangs, hit squads, politicians in the pay of the different groups, and so on. By all accounts that's the situation

251

today. The gangs have more power than the politicians in some parts of the old Soviet Union."

"I was reading somewhere the other day that Cyprus is the place they all want to go to," said Charlie thoughtfully. "Sun and sand and unlimited vodka."

"And no questions asked. Yes, I read that too. Apparently they tip better than the Brits too, which is a bit humiliating. But they've been interested in London as well. They've been cut off for so long that they probably imagine it's still swinging — upbeat instead of deadbeat like it actually is. Quite clearly Mills was going way over the line in providing false documentation for them, setting up connections with all sorts of people in organised crime and specialised crime in this country. By the time he died this was one of the main planks in his business, presumably bringing in most of his money. But I don't think that's what we're interested in."

"What I'm interested in is: who was Stephen Mills?" said Charlie.

Oddie mimed a conjuror drawing a rabbit from a hat.

"And here is your answer: Stojan Milosevic."

"That's a surname you hear rather a lot of these days."

"Yes — I don't think they're related. I don't have a lot of details yet, but what I have says that he had an English mother, who came back to this country when her marriage to a Yugoslav broke down sometime in the early seventies, and he came with her — then in his late teens."

"Hence the perfect but rather precise English," said Charlie.

"Exactly. And the impression we've been getting that he's risen without trace."

"If we're not interested in the Russian Mafia side of his operations —"

"Not just Russian: Polish, Bulgarian, you name it."

"Then what are we interested in?"

"The business of arranging the illegal entry of anyone from Eastern Europe who could afford the hefty sums involved."

Charlie nodded. The thought that that was the connection with Stanko had crossed his mind.

"Ah . . . Does that mean that Stanko, Silvio — oh, I've just thought: we never had a surname for him —"

"Nor a Christian name either. I think I've found an identity for him. If I'm right he's Milan Vico, a Bosnian Serb, who was a student at Zagreb but was desperate to get out to avoid being drawn into the civil war. His family had Moslem connections, but he had — sorry, has — an uncle who is prominent in the struggle on the Serb side: a fearsome fanatic, by the sound of it. Somehow or other his family scraped together the money to get him out. Naturally a lot of Mills's business was done with Yugoslavia, and his name was known in an underground sort of way — particularly in business and student circles. Contact was made, and he managed to get Vico into this country in late ninety-two."

"How?"

"Details are never given in these papers, or almost never. They're revealing in every other way, but not that one. Probably the arrangements were all made by phone. The reason I think this man is Stanko is that he's been in contact with him recently — about six weeks ago — when he was then said to be in Scarborough."

"Promising. What was the contact about?"

"About getting three of his cousins into the country."

"Ah. Again no details given, I suppose?"

"Not about method, not even about the sums of money involved, though there is something about the method of payment. Mills and Vico had met to sort out the details of the operation, but payment was to be handed to someone outside the Scarborough Town Hall. The description fits Brian Ferrett."

Charlie nodded, instinct confirmed.

"Good to have him tied to this side of the business. There might have been difficulties otherwise. I'm beginning to get a picture here. If I'm right, this boy's grievance against Mills could be not some long-ago crime or double-cross, but something very recent indeed."

"Yes — it's beginning to sound rather horrible. But of course it could be just what you call a double-cross: Mills taking the money and then not delivering the goods on the cousins."

"That doesn't sound like the way Mills built up his business. Delivering the goods is precisely what you would have to do to be as successful as he was. And the description of Stanko's reaction to him doesn't really square with that."

The door opened and a uniformed constable came in and handed Charlie a package.

"That came for you from BBC North. Are they giving you the token black part in *The Bill*?"

"That's ITV, you ignorant sod. The best I can hope for is a thirty-second slot on *Crimewatch UK*."

He took out a tape, slotted it into the video, and the two men drew up chairs and began watching. By judicious use of the fast forward button Charlie avoided stories about the dire economic statistics just announced and the government's latest U-turns on education and crime. The item they were waiting for came sixth on the BBC's order of priorities.

"Customs officials and police were called to Southampton this morning when suspicious sounds were heard from a freight container being unloaded from a Liberian-registered merchant ship. When the container was opened they found two men dead from dehydration and starvation, and a third in a very weak state. He has since died in hospital. Police say they believe the men were from Eastern Europe, possibly Yugoslavia. In the fourth round of the F.A. Cup . . ."

Charlie pushed the rewind, and for a moment the men looked at the stark picture of the reddish-brown container on the wharf in Southampton.

"Poor buggers," said Charlie. "What a way to go."

"There we have it," said Oddie sombrely. "The motive."

There was silence as they both considered this.

"Yes," said Charlie at last. "But the motive for what? For the beating-up or the murder?"

Oddie shifted in irritation in his seat.

"Both, surely. You're not saying it's insufficient motive for murder, are you? It doesn't look that way to me. The fight becomes nasty and it leads to murder."

"Maybe. What do the forensic people say?" Mike Oddie shuffled through his papers.

"Blah, blah . . . There's not much more than in the preliminary report we had earlier. . . . Cutting through the jargon we come to . . . Oh here it is. Evidence of a fight of some duration, leading to bruising and cuts. The cuts were the source of the bleeding we found some distance away from the body, so the fight had gone on over a considerable area, as Mills tried desperately to get away. Just as we thought."

"Who needs forensics? Exactly. What then?"

"At some stage Mills collapsed, probably unconscious. Then at some subsequent point of time his throat was cut — source of the considerable amount of blood found under the upper part of his body — surprise, surprise."

"Any indication of the time difference between the end of the attack and the murder?"

"Not directly. To be fair, how could they know? But they do seem to think there could well be one — I think from the bleeding from the *other* wounds under the body."

"Nothing to indicate, then, that the attacker was the murderer?"

"No," said Oddie, irritation in his voice. "Why should we look elsewhere? You enjoy playing devil's advocate I know, but you seem to be placing an awful lot of weight on Yussef's statement that Stanko — Vico — wasn't the type to be a murderer. But he was his friend. He would say that."

"I don't like the idea of his going away from the body — or even just standing there thinking — then suddenly deciding to murder him."

"But that could be *exactly* how it happened," said Oddie, banging a fist on the desk. "He waited for him to come out from the church party, then attacked him in his rage at what he had done to his cousins. When he went away and thought about it he realised that Mills was likely to shop him and that it would be better if he finished him off."

"So he went back, having conveniently a knife in his pocket, and slit his throat? I suspect that when you think about it, Mike, you're not going to like that any more than I do. For a start, it's almost inconceivable Mills would shop him, because it would draw attention to why he was attacked. Stanko said precisely that to Yussef when he went back to Pizza Pronto. If he left him alive, one option would have been to lie low for a few days to see if the police were brought in. By killing him he would make sure he had to disappear, because the police were in with a vengeance. It's a case a defence lawyer could find any number of holes in."

"Either way, we've got to get our hands on the boy. You'd agree about that?"

"Of course."

"We've got some descriptions, but we need a more detailed one. And it would be good if we could find someone who'd co-operate with an artist on an Identi-Kit picture. Would your Mrs Sheffield, do you think?"

"She's not mine, and I don't know her all that well, but no — I don't think she would."

"Then maybe our best bet is the woman who runs the guesthouse in Scarborough. There's every reason for her to be helpful. Or Gabrielli at Pizza Pronto."

Charlie said thoughtfully: "We keep coming back to Mrs Sheffield. I wonder if Stanko has communicated with her. If only we could have put a bug on her telephone."

"You know damned well we couldn't. Do you think they were so close that he would have?"

"I got the impression that they feel very affectionately towards each other, in a non-sexual sort of way. That's how the daughter

saw it too. Yes, I think he might have con-
tacted her. And if she felt pretty confident
he'd got away, there's a chance she might
open up a bit on the subject."

Oddie looked dubious.

"Not to incriminate him, surely?"

"I'm not wanting to incriminate him. I just
want to get at the truth."

"Christ, you sound a prig. Like someone
in a very old-fashioned TV police series."

Charlie smiled wryly.

"Thanks. I'll remember you said that the
next time you get on your moral high horse.
Getting back to Mrs Sheffield. We've got
to remember that she has other connections
with Mills. She'd always disliked him and
distrusted him, and according to Selena
Meadowes she'd done something that Mills
took so seriously that he wanted to get back
at her. She's been very quiet about that."

"Well, I suppose she would, wouldn't she?
But she's not going to be able to stay quiet
about it."

"I wouldn't bet on that. I think she'd be
very good at staying quiet if she dug her
heels in. Anyway, it's probably nothing to
do with the murder."

"You are on her side, aren't you? You've
got no grounds for saying that. At the very
least it's one little piece in the puzzle. And

it could be a very important piece indeed. She left the party early, didn't she?"

"Yes."

"On her own?"

Charlie tried to remember her words.

"I don't think she said so specifically, but I think all the rest of her family stayed till later."

"There you are then. Now, before we go, let's review the evidence, and let's go by your scenario. At some stage towards the end of the party Mills leaves and walks home, as he was likely to do, living close and having been drinking. Stanko (let's call him that) is waiting for him, probably surprises him, and beats him up — the beating going on for some time, Mills trying to get away, but eventually being left unconscious. After Stanko goes back to Pizza Pronto and prepares to disappear again, someone comes along, sees who it is lying there, and, having the wherewithal to do it, cuts his throat. Is that it?"

"Pretty much so," admitted Charlie.

"Well, if you don't like my scenario, I sure as hell don't like yours."

They split up again, Charlie to pressure Rosemary Sheffield on the question of her past relationship with Stephen Mills, Oddie to prepare a detailed description and if possible an Identi-Kit portrait of Milan Vico.

"But press Mrs Sheffield for a good description too," he said to Charlie.

"I'll come the heavy," said Charlie, with no intention of doing so.

When he got to the vicarage it was Rosemary who answered the door. But as he stepped into the shabby hall her son appeared from the kitchen.

*"Again?"* he said, in his prematurely plummy voice. "You're not persecuting my mother, are you?"

"I wasn't intending to," said Charlie amiably. "Are you?"

"Oh Mark, don't be absurd," said Rosemary. The young man opened his mouth, stood there with it open for a second, then thought better of it and turned back to the kitchen.

"I've been perfectly beastly to poor Mark," Rosemary said, leading Charlie into the sitting room. "The other day I called him a pompous little prat."

"He is a pompous little prat, isn't he?"

Rosemary giggled, then obviously felt bad about giggling.

"Oh yes, he is. But whether calling him that is the best way of curing him is another matter."

"If it doesn't work I can't think what will."

"Anyway, he's now very wary of me. I'm glad you've called, as a matter of fact. I've heard from Stanko, you see."

"I thought you might have."

"Now that I know he's got right away I can talk about him more freely."

"Does that include giving me a good description of him?"

She looked at him steadily.

"No it doesn't," she said, without hesitation.

"You're determined to hinder the police in their investigations?"

"Now you sound like a pompous prat. I'm simply not going to help them."

"Even if I tell you that he beat up Mills very severely and left him for dead?"

"I know he did — though actually he was far from dead when he left him. I also know the reason for the fight."

"Three dead or dying illegal immigrants in Southampton."

"Ah — you've got there. I suppose you were bound to. . . . It's too horrible. I hadn't looked at the Sunday papers, and I've only just read the story."

"Nevertheless —"

Rosemary shook her head vigorously.

"As far as I'm concerned there is no 'nevertheless.' What he did is quite understandable."

"I suppose it was Stanko himself who told you he didn't kill him?"

"Yes, it was. And I believe him."

Charlie thought for a moment, then said: "I don't know that I disbelieve him myself."

"Good. But I suppose you'll be going after him and trying to send him back to Yugoslavia?"

"Yes."

"Doesn't that worry you?"

Charlie nodded.

"Some aspects of my job worry me. I expect some aspects of your husband's job worry him. I'd guess it's true of most people who do difficult work."

"That's sophistry. Sending him back would be cruel and wrong. Anyway, you'll do it without any help from me."

"I guessed I would. But you're willing to talk about him? I heard a bit from your daughter, but I'd rather hear it from you. How did the relationship develop in Scarborough?"

"I've thought about that." She looked down, trying to find words, then straight at him again. "You've seen Mark — poor Mark. I'm afraid I've got to the point, without realising it, where I thoroughly dislike my own son. Awful, isn't it? I can only hope it passes, but that will probably happen only if Mark gets out of the phase he's going through. Anyway I think that Stanko — such a nice boy, so quiet and pleasant, and such a sad background — I think he was suddenly there as some sort of substitute son. Certainly I felt motherly towards him."

"Did he tell you about his background?"

"A little, yes. He showed me photographs of his wife and their baby. It seemed so sad, so pathetic, so unnecessary in this day and age. He said that his family was all intermarried, and it was like fighting against a part of yourself. One night he broke down and was sobbing on my shoulder. That sounds like a May–October romance, doesn't it? That's what they tried to spread around the parish, but it wasn't true. It was me in need of a son, if anything, not me in need of a lover."

"Then what happened? He suddenly turned up here?"

"Yes — literally on the doorstep."

"You had no doubts about helping him?"

"No. Why should I?"

"You knew he had no papers?"

"Yes, he told us that on the first evening."

"It made no difference?"

"No," said Rosemary. "Not for either of us."

"Either of you," said Charlie, taking this in. "So you and your husband found him the job at Pizza Pronto. You didn't know of any connection between him and Mills then?"

"Not the slightest idea. His name never came up. At least, now I think about it, when we were looking for a job for him Gi— someone did mention Dark Satanic. We should have twigged, maybe, but we didn't. Of course I got inklings, or rather stronger indications than that, at the party, but the first hard information I had was when Stanko telephoned this morning."

"Did Mills's activities surprise you?"

"*No.*" She thought, trying to put her instincts into words. "You know, calling him Dark Satanic Mills was a joke, but like a lot of jokes there was a serious judgment behind it. There always seemed about him a total lack of moral sense — that in addition to the fact that I just found him, well, *yucky.*"

"But he was a member of your husband's congregation."

Rosemary laughed.

"I don't see what that's got to do with anything. There are a lot of thoroughly dislikable people in my husband's congregation."

"OK, OK — point taken."

"Though I have to say I did find him the *most* dislikable."

"You didn't have to . . . fend him off at any time?"

"Good Lord, no. I think he knew perfectly well how I felt about him. If he didn't, then I wasted a lot of body language and facial language."

"Never even had to slap him down?"

"No."

"What do you know about his home life?"

She gave a moue of distaste at the thought.

"Not very much. I suspect he didn't *have* very much. There's a rather sad little woman sitting there, but mostly he was out and about, making contacts and money. She had had very little to do with us at church in recent years. But her father — old 'Onions' Unwin — was a faithful member. A roaring hot gospeller in his time, and nonconformist, but more respectable with old age. Mills had a lot to do with him and ran his business for a while. They'd usually come to church together."

"Not recently?"

"I believe he's pretty infirm at the moment, and a little bit senile. That was the impression I got the last time I saw him."

"When was that?"

"Oh maybe a year or so ago. He and Dorothy were walking in Herrick Park. He looked so lost and uncertain. I tried to be sympathetic, said he must have a lot of time on his hands now the business was sold, but he just said, 'What? what?' like the mad George III and seemed — well, like him, gaga."

"And what about her? As a person."

"As I said, I very seldom see her, but if you were to press me I'd say she's a woman — was a woman — locked in an unhappy marriage and for some reason seeing no way out for herself. Maybe all I'm saying is that that's how I'd feel if I was married to him, but I don't think so. That said, I don't get the impression that she is a woman who is naturally happy or hopeful. Before she was married she went with her father to the Baptist Church which has closed down now. The impression she gave was that she was a bit put-upon — by him then, later by her husband."

"She didn't have a wide circle of friends?"

"Hardly any, that I know of."

"Why do you think Mills — by the way, his real name was Milosevic —"

"Milosevic! So there was a Yugoslav connection, was there? How interesting."

"Why do you think he was a regular churchgoer?"

"I don't know. I often wondered. It wasn't

as though he was likely to meet an enormous number of business contacts there. He had the Rotary for that. One thing it could give him, though, was respectability. Perhaps with his lack of background — English background, anyway — that was what made it worthwhile for him: something to belong to, something to be said to belong to by people who mattered. Instead of being the Balkan on-the-make adventurer that he was, people mentioned him as a churchgoer — a sober, respectable English type. Though the other side always shone through, as far as I was concerned."

"Did the Church also give him a wife?"

"I don't really remember the sequence of events. We talked about this before. It seems to me he was always thick with Dorothy's father right from the first, but whether he met Dorothy through him or earlier I just don't know. You'd have to ask her."

"Was his grudge against you something to do with the church?"

"We just didn't like each other," said Rosemary, unfazed. "He didn't have a grudge against me."

"He told someone he did."

She looked at him with a blankness that he could have sworn was genuine.

"A *grudge?*"

"The burden of his remark was that you'd done him an injury, and he wasn't going to forget it."

"Done him an injury?" She shook her head, frowning. "I'm sure that can't be right. I'm not conscious of ever doing that. *Who* says he said that?"

"I can't tell you. But part of the paying back was spreading the story about you and Stanko in Scarborough."

"Really? I thought . . . Never mind. He was always very supportive to my face about the parish rows. Told me to fight the old cats — that sort of thing."

"Maybe that was part of the working out of the grudge — keeping the pot boiling."

"Maybe. Maybe it was part of the two-facedness that amused him. But the question is: what was the grudge to start with? I can't think of anything."

"Will you go on thinking?" asked Charlie, getting up to go. "It's probably quite marginal, but then again —"

"Of course . . ." She looked at him closely. "You are telling the truth about Stanko, aren't you? That you haven't made up your mind about his guilt or innocence?"

"Oh yes, I'm telling the truth. I feel we still haven't come to grips with the question of the knife. If Stanko had a knife on him, why did he have a long and vicious fight with Mills without thinking of using it? Apparently he had him unconscious on the ground before the idea occurred to him."

"I agree, that doesn't make sense. And by the way he told me he certainly wasn't carrying one."

"I'll report that, for what it's worth," said Charlie equably. "I think you're a bit biassed. I'm not, but I'm trying to fit the pieces into a sensible pattern. Equally difficult: who could have come along fully prepared to cut somebody's throat."

"Any woman — say a student — could carry a knife, after all the attacks on women in this area. A woman walking across Herrick Park at night could well feel the need for one as protection."

"She'd be a lot better advised *not* to walk across Herrick Park at night, but to stick to the lighted streets."

"People don't always do the sensible thing," said Rosemary, "particularly young people."

"It's something we'll look into. Certainly there may be a lot of women — women of all ages — who might have a grievance against Stephen Mills."

"I can well imagine," said Rosemary grimly.

"On the other hand, in spite of all the scare stories about crime in the press, this country is still a place where the ordinary, law-abiding citizen does not go around carrying a knife."

"Have you thought that Stephen Mills might have been carrying it himself?" asked Rosemary, then looked as if she wished she hadn't.

# Part III

## *Dorothy*

# CHAPTER SEVENTEEN

# *Getting at the Truth*

When she opened the door she was wearing the same sort of nondescript clothing she had had on the day before: each garment could have been interchanged with no difference made to the overall effect. She seemed to be completely indifferent to the effect made, and this apparently was habitual. This time Charlie looked straight into her deep, dark eyes; but they were no more revealing than they had been the day before. It was like groping through underground caves that were close, stifling, part of an unending chain. There was certainly no sign that Mrs Mills felt fear, or even apprehension, on seeing them at her front door.

"Oh, do you have some news?" she asked, in a dry, low voice. "I'm so glad. There are so many people ringing or calling, and there's almost nothing I can tell them."

She led the way through to the sitting room. She had the curtains pulled in obedience to a largely dead custom — one which perhaps her father had insisted on. Again, they all sat down, none of them very sure of themselves, blinking in the dim light. She put on an expectant face, as if she thought she was about to hear that the case had been solved. Oddie started the questioning.

"Mrs Mills, did you know that your husband carried a knife?"

"Stephen? Oh no, he wouldn't do that. He didn't have any enemies." She caught a look in Oddie's eye and quickly amended her statement. "Of course he may have been carrying one on Saturday night."

Don't underestimate her, Oddie said to himself.

"Why should he carry one on Saturday night?"

"Because he'd be coming home across the park. There have been a lot of nasty incidents in the park at nighttime. Well, you'd both know about that. It would have been just elementary self-protection."

Oddie did not tell her that Forensics had said, on the basis of the fabric in the pocket of Mills's jacket, that the indentations were consistent with his habitually carrying a knife.

"You see, we think that was the murder weapon. One can imagine all sorts of possible scenarios. For example, your husband took out the knife during the fight, he was easily disarmed by his attacker who had martial arts expertise, and this man later picked up the knife and murdered him."

He did not mention the alternative possibility, that the knife was removed from his pocket by someone who knew it was there. Mrs Mills nodded seriously.

"Yes, I see." She dabbed at her eyes with her fist. "It seems so horribly *long*, doesn't it, the whole process. First the fight, and then — *that*."

"Mrs Mills, how much did you know about your husband's business activities?"

She screwed up her face.

"Well, not very much, really, except roughly what he did. I told you all about that. I do remember his excitement when he set the business up. Ten or eleven years ago it must be now. Such a happy time! So much enthusiasm and drive!"

In his mind Oddie took a metaphorical pinch of salt.

"Did you know about the office in number 94 Ilkley Road?"

"Is that where it is? I knew he had some sort of overspill office. It was one of the consequences of success, I think. 'Just off to the second office,' Stephen would say."

"Did you know he was running a sort of sideline to the business from there that was, among other things, bringing illegal immigrants into the country?"

There was a silence. Mrs Mills had been maintaining a hard, bright tone, in keeping with her pretence that she was a recently widowed but loving wife, devoted to her husband and to his activities. She made a last shot at propping up the fiction.

"But that's quite impossible! Stephen was impeccably honest. He was a Rotarian." In spite of the tension Oddie and Charlie almost laughed. Again she saw their reaction and immediately backtracked. "Stephen was a man with a conscience. Ask any of his business associates, anyone in the parish. They all trusted him absolutely."

"Mrs Mills, we *know*. The question is, did you know?"

She tossed her head.

"I certainly did not, and I don't believe it. You're making a terrible mistake. . . . Maybe Brian Ferrett has been doing things Stephen knew nothing about."

"Did you know your husband took women to number 94 as well?" asked Charlie.

"You really have been digging for muck,

haven't you?" Dorothy Mills asked bitterly, but looking down to shield her eyes. "Stephen often needed secretarial assistance. Naturally — they had only one girl at European Opportunities Ltd. I suppose policemen always believe the worst, don't they?"

Charlie had had enough of the pantomime.

"And did you accept that it was just secretarial assistance he was after when he brought girls back here and took them upstairs?" he asked.

"He didn't!" she cried, in a voice that was getting progressively more unconvincing. "What kind of filthy nonsense have you been listening to?"

"Janet Sheffield struck me as a very truthful young lady," Charlie said.

There was a long silence, then Dorothy Mills muttered feebly, "Stephen wasn't perfect. What man is these days?"

"Mrs Mills, bringing your girlfriend home, flaunting her at your wife, and then going upstairs and bedding her is not just 'not being perfect.' I think the time has come for you to be honest with us, don't you?"

Again she sat there, thinking, the ticking clock the only sound in the room. Then she turned to Oddie.

"Could you arrange for someone to be with my father? I should like to make a statement, and that had better be at the police station, hadn't it?"

Oddie slipped out into the hall to radio to headquarters. Charlie sat impassive, but even he was surprised when Mrs Mills turned to him and said almost conversationally: "I think it will be best to tell the truth about him, don't you?"

"It will, much the best. I think you'll find we know a lot of it already."

"I don't think so. Most of it only I can know."

Then she stayed quiet until a car came with the inevitable policewoman to look after the old man. Charlie offered Mrs Mills his arm; she got up from the chair and walked out ahead of them to the car.

When they got to police headquarters in the centre of Leeds, Mrs Mills waited quietly in the outer office, a nondescript lady who could have come in about a lost dog. When Oddie had arranged an interview room she followed him obediently as if she were one. But when all three had sat down and Oddie was getting out a tape, she showed that she had a mind of her own.

"Would you mind if I just told you — told you about me and Stephen and . . . everybody, right from the beginning? Of course you realise that much of what I told you before wasn't true. It will come out much more easily if I tell it my way than questions and answers."

"There may have to be questions if you forget to tell us something we need to know," said Oddie.

"Yes, of course. But otherwise will you let me tell it in my own way?"

"Yes. Certainly we can try it like that." He spoke into the microphone. "Interview with Dorothy Mills, seventeenth of May 1994. Detective Superintendent Oddie and DC Peace present."

She was sitting opposite him, still and collected, apparently perfectly calm. When he had recorded the necessary documentation he gestured to her to go ahead. She thought for a little, swallowed, and then began.

"I lied about how I met Stephen. It was something I liked to put out of my mind — it was so like his usual pickups. I met him in 1978 on a train from London. I was finishing my second term at teachers college, and already I'd decided I wasn't cut out to be a teacher. I was one of those many who aren't, but go on with it because they can't think of anything else to do. I had already more or less decided to get out. Stephen sat opposite me, across the table, and the moment

I saw him I thought he was the handsomest man, the most exciting man, I'd seen in my life. A lot of people have thought that, before and since. When he started to talk to me my heart started to thump like a hammer on an anvil, and I know I blushed scarlet. Stephen was used to having that effect, but he didn't let that show, then. Later he became sort of complacent, and put a lot of women off. He kept the conversation low-key, and before long I calmed down. He got me a cup of tea and a sandwich, and quite soon we weren't talking about the weather or the places we were passing in the train, but about me. Stephen was always very good at getting women to talk about themselves — at least, the sort of women who were attracted to the sort of man he was."

"Tell us something about yourself," said Oddie quietly. She looked surprised.

"Me? Somehow I don't seem to matter in all this. . . . All right, I'll try. I was brought up in what I suppose was a dull, middle-class household. My mother died when I was ten, so I was very close to my father, or perhaps I should say that I thought I was. What Dad had always wanted was a son. He owned a good furniture shop in Abbingley, and was — is — a very committed Christian. Our lives then revolved around the church, which was an evangelical Baptist one. It's gone now. The congregation got older and older, and then died. . . . I was a timid, repressed, not at all charming young woman."

With unfathomably deep eyes, thought Charlie.

"All this I told Stephen, that first meeting, and much more. When he wanted to — when he wanted to learn something — he could just sit quietly, listen intelligently, and hear everything he wanted to hear. By the end of the journey he knew me through and through. I would have felt naked before him, if I had thought like that. As it was, I remembered my manners enough to ask him about himself, though that was not before we drew out of Wakefield. He told me he was from London and was coming to Leeds to start a new job. That was fairly typical of Stephen: he was economical with the facts about himself. There are still large areas of his life about which I know nothing, though that's partly because for a long time I haven't wanted to know, preferred not to. That time he diverted me from the subject by asking for my address. I couldn't believe my ears. It was the first time I'd been asked for my address — and by *such* a man! As I was writing it down, eyes glued to the table to hide disappointment if he refused, I asked him if he'd like to come to supper the next night. He said at once, 'That would be wonderful. You'll be the first people I know in Leeds.' I just felt . . . elated, on a cloud, on a drug trip, if I'd thought like that. Like Cinderella suddenly confronted for the first time with Prince Charming."

She sat there for a moment, lost in memory.

"How did your father take to him?" Charlie asked.

"When I told him, he was suspicious. It was the first time I'd ever asked anyone home, anyone male, anyone young at all, and he said he didn't like his daughter asking to the house a young man she'd just met — he didn't say 'picked up,' but he probably thought it — on a train. But when Stephen came round everything changed. . . . Stephen was very good with men too, you know. Maybe better. He was good at drawing out women, but basically he despised them and thought they were good for only one thing. With men he was in his element: he could talk business, the economic situation, export possibilities, the trade unions — it was all grist to him, and he was very good, very convincing. I should have been bored, I had been a hundred times with that sort of conversation, but I sat there gazing at him fascinated, thinking I understood."

"I suppose they talked about religion too," said Oddie.

"Oh yes. With my father you always got on to religion. Stephen said he was an Anglican. I'm sure he'd thought about it, after our conversation on the train, and he was prepared to be a Christian but he was damned if he was going to be an evangelical nonconformist. After we were married he would go along now and then to the Baptist Church, and he'd ask father along to St Saviour's. Eventually Dad made the changeover completely."

"Why do you think your husband continued going to church?" asked Charlie.

"It was part of his respectable image. He half-realised there was something of the adventurer and gigolo about him, but the Anglican Church built up another side to him in people's minds. He did meet the odd influential person there, but after Dad nominated him for Rotary Club he used that mostly to get contacts. But Rotary Club is not respectable as the Church of England is respectable. People laugh at it a bit, as they do the Masons, and they think it's full of back scratchers."

She paused, having allowed herself to be sidetracked. She tried to get back to those early days.

"It was the happiest time of my life. Stephen was working with a building society, but he was anxious to start his own business. Dad was captivated by him and willing to do everything in the way of helping him and introducing him to people. In the little spare time he had we went places together — plays, concerts, church do's of one sort or another. After a respectable amount of time — after the middle-class, English amount of time — we got engaged. Dad was over the moon. So was I. We didn't sleep together. It seems funny to think of now. Stephen was acting his part well, but perhaps overacting a little. Did you realize he was only uncertainly English? He lived in Yugoslavia till he was seventeen. Of course now I know he must have been getting what he wanted from someone, perhaps many, but at the time I knew or suspected nothing. Dad gave me away at St Saviour's, and I think it was the happiest moment of his life as well as mine." She paused, then suddenly spat out: "I burnt the wedding pictures later. I couldn't bear to look at them. I couldn't even say I'd been sold. I'd sold myself."

There was silence in the room for a moment.

"How soon did things start going wrong?"

Oddie asked gently. She answered him only indirectly.

"I once read about Lord Byron, and how he told his wife on their wedding night that he'd only married her for revenge. In my case it wasn't revenge, it was because of all Dad could offer, but he did make things pretty clear right from the start. . . . I wasn't very good in bed. Not at all what he had been used to. He wasn't gentle or understanding — he was contemptuous. He just gave up on me as soon as he'd had me. By the end of the honeymoon he wasn't bothering to hide his impatience to get home and get down to what really interested him in life: making money. He felt sure that, now we were married, Dad would be willing to make a big investment in him, and he was right. By the end of the honeymoon I knew I was an irrelevance in his life, a means, a steppingstone. It hurt."

"Did you both put up a front for your father's benefit?" Charlie asked.

"Oh yes — at first. Later on Stephen stopped bothering, because Dad didn't notice. I'd been around all his life, and though he'd been forced to make do with what he'd got he'd never thought much to daughters. It was Stephen who fascinated him, and before long I stopped interesting him at all. He set Stephen up in business and was taken with the whole idea of European Opportunities Ltd. He'd come round to our house, Stephen would be round at his. Meanwhile the marriage became nothing more than a facade, a shell, a charade — call it what you will."

"But you didn't think of leaving him?"

"I *thought*. . . . But what would I do? Go back to live with Dad? I'd have seen more of Stephen there than if I'd stayed married to him. Get a job? But what could I do? I had no training, no experience, no confidence. And after a time Dad began to fail with very bad arthritis. I could see it happening, and in the end we moved into his house, our old home, and built a little flat on the back for him, and that seemed about as satisfactory a solution as I could hope for. I wasn't *happy*, but it worked."

She stopped. The men thought they'd asked too many questions, and they let her continue in her own fashion.

"I said the marriage was a shell. That was true for a long time. We would have the odd meal together, almost by accident, and that was it. Otherwise a meal was always there when he came in, and some days we hardly saw each other, hardly exchanged a word. That was perfectly satisfactory as far as I was concerned. Of course we didn't sleep together

— the mere thought of it nauseated me —
and I knew he had plenty of substitutes: paid,
casual, sometimes a bit more than that, but
never anything involving real feeling. Stephen
was incapable of real feeling. Mostly what
was involved was humiliation. I know because
. . . There was a change, you see. For a
time he was so busy running two businesses,
Dad's and his own, that our marriage more
or less ceased to exist. Eventually even Dad
would have noticed that, but he was becoming
more inward-looking, not noticing anything
except his immediate comforts. Then Stephen
got rid of the furniture business, and I think
around that time he started getting into all
sorts of dodgy businesses — organised crime
in the East European countries, and so on.
That was much more exciting than any boring
old furniture firm, and more profitable too.
It gave spice to his life, he began to relish
living on the edge of danger. It brought out
the buccaneer in him."

She looked up and straight at them.

"It spilled over into the marriage. Indif-
ference, living our own lives separately,
wasn't enough any more. It was as if he resented the fact that he'd trapped himself in
a loveless, unexciting marriage when all the
time there were these more thrilling ways
of making money and getting on that he

hadn't thought about when he used me to do that." She paused, and her mouth involuntarily went into a little moue. "He began to be around more, to torment me. He would sit at the breakfast table and read aloud from love letters begging him to leave his boring wife and go off with whoever it was. 'Why don't you?' I'd say. He began bringing girls home — all sorts of girls — and flaunting them in front of me before taking them upstairs to make love. . . . What a phrase: 'make love'! . . . I hated that, I have to admit. I couldn't cope with that, and I couldn't tell you why to this day. Some of them were tarts, but some of them were really nice girls like Janet Sheffield, and that was worse. I was sorry for them. . . . One day he raped me. I don't want to go into that. I told him that if it ever happened again I'd murder him."

"Did it?"

"No. He knew I meant it."

"Why didn't you turn him out of the house?"

"His own house? Dad had made it over to him the same time as he'd handed over the business to him. . . . Oh, I know there are ways, but I've never been a strong person. Not determined or single-minded. I felt trapped. If Dad had died I'd have done something, but he's still well apart from the arthritis, though his mind has been going for some time. Stephen found that mightily amusing, of course. Now and again he'd tell people at church about silly things Dad had said or done, exaggerating, to show what he'd sunk to. . . . I'd almost stopped going to church myself soon after we were married."

"Why?"

"I don't know. I don't think I'd lost my faith, at least not then, but I didn't want to be part of Stephen's *using* religion. It demeaned it. Stephen didn't have a faith! He didn't even have a moral code, not even the faintest ethical barrier beyond which he wouldn't go. . . . Stephen would do *any*thing. . . . Shall I tell you about Saturday evening?"

"Please."

She paused, collecting her thoughts.

"I had no intention of going to the church party. I never went to any function with Stephen unless he forced me, which he did now and then when the whim took him, mainly to establish respectable-married-man credentials. But it was true that the cat was missing. I'm very fond of Moggs. Sometimes he just sits there *looking* at Stephen, as if judging him, deciding he's lower than an insect he wouldn't waste his time catching. I like that. . . . Stephen came in to change about seven.

There'd been a phone call earlier — a foreign man, sounding very upset. He didn't leave a message, but I told Stephen about it. He just shrugged. He went out shouting good-bye to Dad: 'Bye, Dad — have a good time.' His idea of humour." She frowned in thought. "That was the last time I'll ever hear his voice."

She paused, as if trying to order events in her own mind.

"During the evening I watched a bit of tele-vision, listened to Radio Three. I kept going out into the garden and calling for Moggs, then along the road too. He's a neutered tom, but he's a real prowler when the mood takes him. I always worry when he goes missing because we're so close to the Ilkley Road. I lied about his never crossing that. Once we found him in Herrick Park. Anyway I got Dad his nightcap. He always has Ovaltine around half past nine. Then I went out again, back home, out again. Eventually, after the ITV news, I decided to go across to Herrick Park. It was silly, I know: the only sensible thing when a cat is lost is to wait for him to come home. But when it's the only thing you've got, almost . . ."

"And that was — when?"

"Getting on for half past ten. The evening news had been at ten past ten, and I'd heard the item about the illegal immigrants who had died. It was quite horrible. I'd wondered whether Stephen was involved. He was, wasn't he?"

"Yes, he was."

"I knew that much about what he was up to, you see. Anyway, I walked down to the Ilkley Road, crossed it, keeping my eye skimmed all the time for Moggs, dreading to see him hit by a car or already lying dead in the road. It's a horrible sight, isn't it, a dead cat in the middle of the road? They're so fragile. . . . The edge of the park is only five or six minutes from our house, and as soon as I got there I started calling for Moggs. It was dark, of course, and I was rather afraid. It's not a place most people would willingly go on to at night, particularly women. First I kept near the road, close to the lights, but then I thought that defeated the purpose of looking for him because Moggs certainly didn't need street lights. . . . Anyway, I'd gone away from the road and was over towards the tennis courts when I jumped with fear. I'd thought I heard shouts."

"Where from?"

"From the other end of the park — from the edge of the clump of trees on the rise. It was the fight, of course. I was terrified. All those nasty incidents on the park — you know about them, of course — came flooding into my mind. I started to hurry to the road, but the quickest route to it didn't take me away from the fight but towards it. And the fight seemed to be coming in that direction. They were coming away from the trees and towards the road, one running, the other following. And as I looked and began to hurry away in the other direction I thought that one of the men looked like Stephen."

She stopped, remembering. Oddie and Charlie left her a moment or two to collect her thoughts. In those moments Charlie suddenly asked himself: why is she telling us this? He could not find an answer.

"What did you do?" Oddie asked at last, gently.

"I hid behind a tree. I thought, you see, that I probably wasn't in any danger. I thought it was most likely a husband or a boyfriend of someone that Stephen had . . . To tell you the truth I was pleased he was getting what he deserved. I wanted to watch it." She looked at them, not pleading, but to see if they understood. "I'm sorry, it sounds disgusting but that's the truth of it. . . . The other man was doing all sorts of things with his outstretched hands and arms — like men I've seen on television slicing bricks in half and that kind of thing. He was using his feet too — like a modern ballet. Stephen was crying out. I knew it was him by now. Then suddenly there was a blow to the head and it was all over. Stephen was lying stretched out on the ground, and the other man was running away in the direction of the Ilkley Road."

"What did you do?"

"I stood there under a tree for a moment or two, uncertain what to do. The sensible thing would have been to go straight home. I don't know why I didn't, or why . . . I walked over to where Stephen was lying. He was quite unconscious, and I could see blood on him. But he was breathing. I stood there looking down on him. A great wash of feeling came over me, as if I was drowning, and everything he had ever done, to me, to Dad, to others, came over me like a big wave. . . . I can't explain the feeling, but it seemed somehow too little. . . . After *all* he'd done: the hateful things, the criminal things, the humiliating things. I think it must have been what the victims feel when a judge imposes a very light sentence on someone who has done really dreadful things to them. It was how he'd treated *everyone* that I was thinking of, not just me. The heartlessness, the hypocrisy, the double-dealing. It seemed too little. . . . I can't explain what I did, *why* I did it. I don't think I thought. But somewhere in the back of my mind there may have been the idea that if I didn't do it *now*, then so good an opportunity would never come again. . . . I bent down and took from his pocket the little knife I knew he always carried. It's small but very sharp — deadly. I pressed the catch and the blade sprung forward. He stirred. I knew if I was going to do it, it had to be then. I bent down and slit his throat."

There was utter silence in the little room. Oddie said, at last, "Just like that?"

"Just like that. Without any emotion."

"What did you do then?"

"I stood for a moment watching him die. Only that way could it seem *enough*." She looked at them to see if she had shocked them, but they remained impassive. "Then I walked back across the park on my way home, calling to Moggs all the time. I slipped the knife down a drain when I got to the road, and I held a scarf in my hand to hide the fact that my hands were bloody. Moggs was on the front doorstep when I got home — it's always the way, isn't it? I ran water into an old plastic bowl and washed the blood off myself. I've seen all those police things on television, you know, and I knew they can trace the tiniest bit of blood left in a sink. Then I went out again and disposed of the bowl in a skip, and the scarf too. Then I went home and began to prepare for all the pretence that would be necessary the next day. I decided I had to at least pretend to be the devoted wife. If I'd told the truth about him and me I'd be the first to be suspected. And what would Dad do if I was sent to prison? So I thought hard about what I'd say to you when you came. But I slept — I slept very well. I didn't have any doubts or pricks of conscience, and I haven't had since either. That's odd, isn't it? Someone who used to be a regular churchgoer. I suppose it's a measure of the sort of man Stephen was. . . . Is that enough? Will your tape have all that?"

"Yes, that's enough," said Oddie. He moved to switch off the tape, but Charlie put out his hand to stop him. He still hadn't found the answer to his question. He looked at the woman opposite, at her only good feature — her deep eyes, almost black: eyes that looked at him and told him nothing, except that what they probably concealed was pain, loneliness and the emptiness of being unloved. It seemed almost an act of cruelty to ask her anything more, but Charlie felt he had to chance his arm.

"Why did they call your father 'Onions'?" he asked.

She looked at him, quickly and sharply.

"What? What do you mean? Why on earth are you asking me about that?"

"His nickname in Abbingley. 'Onions.' Was it because he could cry at will at those revivalist meetings he went in for? Real, wet tears like he turned on for us?"

"I don't understand. Why are you saying those nasty things about him?"

"When did he find out that Stephen had sold his beloved business, and when did he start hating him as much as you did?"

"He didn't! He loved him!"

"Oh no, he didn't. Because it wasn't your cat you went to look for on Herrick Park, was it? It was your father. And by the time you found him he'd killed your husband."

The great eyes suddenly filled with tears and she fell forward on to the table, racked with sobs. They waited, listening to her barely distinguishable words. The only ones Charlie thought he could make out were, "Why did you let me go on? How did you know?"

# CHAPTER EIGHTEEN

# *Envoi*

*I*t was several weeks before Charlie had any conversation about the case with Rosemary Sheffield. When he did he said rather more than, strictly, he ought to have done, mainly because in the course of the case he had come not only to like her but to trust her too. And it was not as though there was any prospect of the case coming to court.

It happened one Sunday, when he was jogging around Herrick Park, as he generally did on days off, though in no fanatical spirit. Running down the gentle incline from the small wooded area, very near the place where Stephen Mills's body had lain, he saw the Reverend Sheffield making pedantic little dabs at the door handle of his car with a cloth; and he saw Rosemary come out, a puppy in her arms. She kissed her husband and raised her hand as he drove off on his way to morning service. Charlie in turn raised his hand to her, then turned aside from his usual route and ran over to her. They both knew perfectly well what they were going to talk about, and when Rosemary had set the puppy down safely in the front garden they sat against the garden wall of the vicarage that abutted the road, Charlie panting slightly.

"They say the old man has been institutionalised — is that true?" Rosemary asked. Charlie nodded.

"Yes. It was the devil's own job to get a place for him at a secure establishment, but in the end, one had to be found. These days it's no good being mentally ill — you have to have cut someone's throat as well."

"Dorothy's had a lot of well-wishers from the congregation."

Charlie laughed cynically.

"I *bet* she has! They left her pretty well alone when she was the neglected and mistreated wife."

"Yes, we all did. To be fair, I was as guilty as anyone."

"And to be fair on the other side, she didn't want to have much to do with a church that could have Stephen as an honoured member."

Rosemary nodded.

"Yes, that always worried me too, but what could you do? He was, to all intents and purposes, an upright citizen. . . . She told one of the well-wishers that she had confessed to the murder. Is that true?"

"Yes, it is."

"I believe a lot of people do that during murder enquiries. Is that why you didn't just accept her confession?"

"We always look closely at confessions. They have to stand up in court. . . ." Charlie pulled himself up. He was starting to sound like a PR man. "But, well, the fact is that we very nearly did accept it, at least for a time. The fact is that most of what she told us the first time we talked to her was lies. The devoted husband and son-in-law stuff was the only thing she could think of to shield her father — and herself, by then his accomplice. Most of what she told us during the second interview was true. But not all. And there were significant gaps. You know, you sit there listening to someone confess, and if everything fits neatly with the facts — and it did in her confession, mainly because it was very *nearly* the truth — then your mind doesn't make the leap away from the facts to ask itself the bigger questions."

"Such as?"

"Such as: why is she making this confession at all? We had nothing on her, beyond her lying about her relationship with her husband

— perfectly easily explained, when her husband had just been murdered. But we no sooner confronted her with those lies than she upped and confessed."

"She's such a depressed and depressing little thing that I think I'd have decided that she just didn't have the gumption to go on lying any more."

"I'm not sure I agree with the assessment," said Charlie thoughtfully. "Maybe you don't know her very well."

Rosemary nodded.

"I don't. I admit it."

"There's more *there* than you allow for. Though what exactly it *is* I'm not sure I could say. But however you assess her character, I would have expected her to go on protesting her innocence to protect the position of her father, who depended on her. That's one person she loves, even if that love isn't returned with any great enthusiasm. As they always say: he's all she's got. Her thought, her solicitude, were all for him. And yet her confession, her arrest, would leave him alone. So at one point I asked myself: why?"

"And the answer?"

"The only convincing answer I could come up with was that the alternative was worse."

"His arrest and trial?"

"Yes. Of course it hasn't come to that because he's been found unfit to plead."

There was a hesitancy in Charlie's manner that made Rosemary ask, "And are you happy with that?"

"Happy? Oh yes, happy we don't have to put an eighty-year-old on trial and imprison him for the few years he has left in a thoroughly unsuitable institution."

"Well, to put it another way: do you think it was the right decision?"

Charlie sat in the dim sunlight, pondering.

"The psychiatrist was the best of the bunch we have to call on: sensible, down to earth, not one of those who's crazier than the patient. He examined Unwin over a two-month period. At the end he was willing to declare him unfit to plead. Everyone breathed a sigh of relief."

"But it wasn't an open-and-shut matter?"

"No, it wasn't. He had several reservations which he put in his report, no doubt to satisfy his professional conscience. There were aspects of Unwin's behaviour that were not in accordance with the usual progress of Alzheimer's disease or senile dementia. But he was the first to admit that you can't be dogmatic about such things. And the fact is that the idea that Unwin is senile depends on his behaviour since the murder, his daughter's testimony — one of the places where she was lying, I suspect — and a few stories Mills told about him to the St Saviour's congregation. How often had you seen him in the last six or seven years?"

"Just the once — the time I told you about."

"I should think that was true of everyone. His contemporaries had either died off or were in a similar situation to his own. Old people do get forgetful, confuse names, muddle up past and present. Mills could no doubt have told true stories about the old man that suggested he was far gone mentally."

"But what makes you think he wasn't?"

"The tears when he heard about Mills's death. First I thought they were genuine grief. But later I heard from you about his nickname, 'Onions.' And I wondered whether this wasn't a satirical commentary on his being able to produce tears at will."

"It was," said Rosemary with relish. "The real waterworks. 'Oh Lord, I have been a great sinner!' with abundant liquid evidence of repentance."

"I thought that might be it."

"Oh, how nice it is to be able to laugh at things like that."

"Anyway, when I thought about the tears when Mills died, I realized that they were turned on in the old, practised way, and they fooled me, for one. I thought it was the most genuine grief I'd seen so far."

"But they *had* been fond of each other. Or rather, old Unwin had been fond of Stephen."

"That's right. But I think things had gone downhill in recent years — probably ever since Unwin stopped being useful to Mills. He'd begun flaunting his women in front of him — we learnt this from . . . one of his girlfriends."

"From Janet. Don't worry — I've guessed about that."

"Well, anyway . . . Unwin was a puritan of the old breed — possibly a fearsome old hypocrite to boot, but he would have been shocked and disgusted. Mills made satirical remarks about his physical and mental condition — we know that from Dorothy. And then he'd learned that his beloved furniture business had been sold off."

"Oh dear. Was that me?"

"I think it might have been. I think that was the grudge he had against you."

"I seem to have had fatal effects in this business."

"If it hadn't been you it could have been anyone. The fact is he only got out when the arthritis was in remission, when he tended to go off on his own. The likelihood was he wouldn't see anyone he knew on those wanderings."

"But the business had been sold without his knowing?"

"Yes. He'd made it over to Mills for tax reasons. When he took it over Mills stipulated that Unwin shouldn't interfere — he shouldn't even go back to his old shop. Actually it was a perfectly sensible condition. It's everyone's nightmare, the chap who had the job before you coming back and sticking his oar in. Unwin was a businessman himself, saw the point, and agreed without a qualm."

"But the business didn't prosper under Stephen?"

"I think it was the recession rather than Mills that sent it into a tailspin. You see all these rather desperate ads, don't you, on television: no interest for the first two years — that kind of thing. Heavy, traditional English furniture is not what people buy when times are hard. When Mills found the shop was making very little money for him, he sold it for what he could get and ploughed the money into his dubious East European activities."

"Bringing in illegal immigrants?"

"That and much, much more."

"But it's hardly a motive for murder, is it?"

"Not by itself. It was cumulative, I think. The old man had loved his business, lived for it and for his religion. He'd welcomed Mills as a son-in-law because he recognised him as a superb businessman who would take over after him. I think when he realised that the firm had been sold when things were difficult, when he realised his son was a common womaniser who had just used religion as a way of sucking up, when he became the butt of his cruel jokes, I think he realised that Mills had been using him for years, had made a complete fool of him. I think for the last few months, maybe years, he'd hated him. Probably it brought him and his daughter closer together than they'd ever been."

"I see. And I suppose the hatred and resentment would have gone on smouldering until the old man died without Stephen being murdered if the opportunity hadn't presented itself."

"Exactly. What *really* happened that night was not that Dorothy Mills came to Herrick Park looking for her cat. In fact, she was on her way up to bed when she saw through a crack in the door that the light was still on in her father's flat. She'd taken him his nightcap more than an hour earlier, and usually he'd have been well in bed by then. When she went in she found he'd gone wandering,

307

as he had more than once before."

"I suppose he could have done that when I saw them on the park, and she'd come and got him."

"Exactly. The park was where he most often came. Now, what Dorothy said had happened to *her* was probably what happened to *him*. He probably told her about it later. He walked over to the park, then wandered around it, and eventually heard and saw the fight from a distance. Whether he recognised his son-in-law we can't say, but when it was over he went to where the man lay, saw it was Stephen . . ."

"Then cut his throat?"

"Yes."

"Just like that?"

"Well, we don't know how long he thought about it or what sort of thought he was capable of. I'm not denying he was old and confused, just that he was senile. Dorothy had by this time come on to the park. She saw the figure of her father in the distance and ran over to him. By then it was already done, and his jacket sleeve was covered with blood. . . . That was another thing that worried me with her account."

"What?"

"Not enough blood. You cut someone's throat and it really spurts blood."

"That must have made getting him home difficult."

"Difficult and dangerous. There's a stretch of well-lighted road between the park and the Ilkley Road, as you know, and she could avoid it only by taking a very long way round, which he probably couldn't manage. She solved it by making her headscarf into a sort of sling, which hid most of the blood. When she got home she washed him clean in a plastic bowl — she knew from those television crime series (isn't television wonderful?) that it is very difficult to get rid of all traces of blood in a modern plumbing system — then went out and disposed of the bowl and the bloody scarf in a skip. Unwin's jacket was the most dangerous thing: she put it in a plastic bag and dumped it in a large bin on the Ilkley Road which she knew was emptied every day. Then all she had to fear was her father giving things away, so she really had to tutor him in how he should behave when the murder came out. He was sharp enough to take her point and follow her direction — a practised old hypocrite, I suspect."

"She seems to have been rather clever."

"Yes. I said I didn't go along with your assessment of her. Granted the situation she was presented with, she showed great presence of mind."

"How *do* you rate her? What kind of person is she?"

Charlie shook his head.

"I don't know. I just can't fathom her. Unloved, neglected by both husband and father, seething with humiliation and resentment. But I don't *feel* her character. Anything I know, I've been *told* by her, which is different. I feel I know what kind of man Mills was by now, but I don't feel I have the same knowledge of his wife."

"People say she's going to move."

"I don't blame her. Though there's always the danger that she'll simply be even more lonely in strange surroundings. Still, there's nothing to keep her here. And she's used to loneliness — probably prefers it."

"Will she have any money?"

"Sure. The house will bring in plenty, even in the current state of the market; and the legitimate side of the business is saleable: it was a good idea, and there will be people who can carry it on. Personally I hope they don't continue to employ Brian Ferrett, but we can't do anything about that."

"Was that Mills's assistant?"

"Yes. In it up to his ears, but we can't charge him."

"Why not?"

"You've probably heard about the Crown

Prosecution Service. These days they don't let us charge anyone unless it's almost one hundred per cent sure we'll get a conviction. It's very frustrating. On Ferrett we had no more than fingerprints in number 94 — that's the place where all the dubious business was transacted — and a description in a letter. We might have had a hope if we'd managed to get hold of Stanko — of Milan Vico."

"Well, I'm very glad you haven't."

"Have you heard from him recently?"

"Just a one-minute phone call to say he's all right. I don't need anything else. I wasn't in love with him, you know."

"I know."

"I was just so sad for him — running away from the fighting, having to leave his wife and baby behind."

Charlie hesitated, shuffled his feet, and then said, "Actually, we know quite a bit about Milan Vico now. Nothing criminal or to his discredit. But we've never had the slightest hint that he was married."

"Oh." For a moment Rosemary was non-plussed. "You mean they were just sympathy getters?"

"Something like that. I expect they were relatives — a sister or a cousin and her child, say — whose photographs he had brought with him."

Rosemary thought and then said, "It doesn't make any difference, you know, not to how I see him. I expect if I were alone in a foreign, hostile country (because that's what this is), I'd make a play for all the sympathy I could get from anyone who seemed kind or well disposed. I didn't befriend him because he was brave and truthful or the soul of honour."

"You befriended him because he was a nice boy and slightly pathetic."

"That's probably true. And as a son substitute."

"How is young Mark?"

"Hmmm. There's been a *slight* improvement. He sometimes stops himself before he makes a horribly pompous remark (I always know what the remark would have been). Or he says, 'I know you'll say I'm being pompous, but — .' I suppose you could say there's been a slight increase in self-knowledge. But I still feel very remote from him."

"Well," said Charlie, sliding off the wall and dusting the seat of his track suit, "I won't apply for the vacant post of son substitute."

"Please don't. I don't see you as one at all. You may be nice, but there's nothing of the pathetic about you."

"Oh, I'm not even nice. And I was — am — a lousy son."

"I don't believe that. Anyway, I certainly wouldn't want pathetic policemen, though a few more nice ones wouldn't go amiss. I'll try to make do with what I've got. Janet's a lovely daughter, I like her boyfriend, and Paul's come out of this best of all: loving and loyal and steadfast — everything a husband should be."

"I notice you don't put the final spit and polish to his car before service any longer."

"No, aren't I awful? One awakening leads to another, I suppose. It suddenly seemed too ridiculous to go on doing it."

"Anyway, I'll take my girlfriend along to St Saviour's to hear him sometime."

"Oh, I didn't say he was a splendid preacher," Rosemary laughed. "Workaday, but no more than that."

Charlie raised his hand. "See you," he said, and crossed the road and started jogging round the perimeter of the park.

There was a watery sun shining now, and Rosemary bent down to pick up her puppy, who had begun throwing himself against the wall. They crossed the road and walked under the trees, the puppy snuffling happily and independently. Rosemary's thoughts were far away. It was here that, for her, things had all started. Not for the main participants, of course. For them the thing had started long ago, probably when Dark Satanic and poor Dorothy had met. But for Rosemary life had changed suddenly here on Herrick Park; and as a consequence her life had become horribly, fatally involved with the affairs of a man she disliked and shrank from. Well, in that her instinct had been right.

How she had so suddenly lost her belief in God was still a mystery to her. The suddenness of its leaving her seemed almost, ridiculously, like an act of God itself. But she did feel, as she walked under the trees, her eye on her lovely new dog, with the everyday activities of the park going on around, that the very suddenness and out-of-the-blueness of its going was an indication that one day, possibly, it would return to her, descend, envelop her with the same odd unpredictability. Sometimes recently she had got as far as hoping that it would.

# ABOUT THE AUTHOR

*R*obert Barnard's most recent novel is *The Masters of the House.* His other books include *A Hovering of Vultures, A Fatal Attachment, A Scandal in Belgravia, A City of Strangers, At Death's Door, The Skeleton in the Grass,* and *Out of the Blackout.* A seven-time Edgar nominee and winner of the Anthony, Agatha, Macavity, and Nero Wolfe awards, he lives in Leeds, England.

We hope you have enjoyed this Large Print book. Other Thorndike Press or Chivers Press Large Print books are available at your library or directly from the publishers. For more information about current and upcoming titles, please call or write, without obligation, to:

Thorndike Press
P.O. Box 159
Thorndike, Maine 04986
USA
Tel. (800) 223-6121 (U.S. & Canada)
In Maine call collect: (207) 948-2962

*OR*

Chivers Press Limited
Windsor Bridge Road
Bath BA2 3AX
England
Tel. (0225) 335336

All our Large Print titles are designed for easy reading, and all our books are made to last.